PITCH DARK

PITCH DARK

RENATA ADLER

ALFRED A. KNOPF   NEW YORK   1983

THIS IS A BORZOI BOOK
PUBLISHED BY ALFRED A. KNOPF, INC.

Copyright © 1983 by Renata Adler

Library of Congress Cataloging in Publication Data
Adler, Renata.   Pitch dark.   I. Title.
PS3551.D63P5   1983   813'.54   83-48133
ISBN 0-394-50374-0

Manufactured in the United States of America
First Edition

For J.

PITCH DARK

I. ORCAS ISLAND

We were running flat out. The opening was dazzling. The middle was dazzling. The ending was dazzling. It was like a steeplechase composed entirely of hurdles.

But that would not be a steeplechase at all. It would be more like a steep, steep climb.

They were shouting, Tell it, big momma, tell it. I mean, the child is only six years old.

Do I need to stylize it, then, or can I tell it as it was?

He knew that she had left him when she began to smoke again.

Look here, you know, I loved you.

I wonder whether he will ever ask himself, say to himself, Well, she wasn't asking all the earth, why did I let her go?

My *back* went up, Viola Teagarden used to say, with a little thrill of self-importance, pride and pleasure, head raised, nostrils flaring, back straightening slightly, as though she had received a small electric charge right through her chair. My *back* went up.

She also spoke with a kind of awe of what she called "my anger," as though it were a living, prized possession, a thoroughbred bull, for instance, to be used at stud, or as a man who has married a beautiful, unpredictably unpleasant woman, far richer and younger than himself, might say "my wife." Leander Dworkin, too, though he hardly knew Viola and in fact despised her, had what he called "my rage." It resembled, sometimes a hothouse of imaginary grievances under lavish cultivation, sometimes a pulse which he measured constantly to see whether, with whom, and to what degree he must be angry, sometimes a source of astonishment and pleasure, sometimes just a horse to be taken for a canter or a gallop on the moors. In times of rage, he wanted nothing to distract or mollify him. Even flattery, for which his appetite was otherwise undiscriminating and enormous, would infuriate him on his way to an apotheosis. A few people humored him in this. They were his friends. Inevitably, it was with one or more of these few friends that he was angry—a source, at first, always of distress, since he broke off with words as harsh as they were capricious, and then, for the long quiet interval that followed, of relief.

To begin with, I almost went, alone, to Graham Island.

He thought of himself, even spoke of himself, as extraordinarily handsome. His hair, which grew to collar length, was reddish. His hairline was receding; his eyes, which blinked constantly over his contact lenses, were the palest blue. Though he was by no means a strikingly ugly man, the source of his belief in his physical beauty seemed to lie in this: that he was tall. Leander Dworkin was the amplifying poet. Willie Stokes was the poet of compression. Both taught poetry, and wrote novels, when we were in graduate school. We met in two improbable seminars, taught by great men. Notions of Paradise, and Sound in Literature. The first was literary utopias, essentially; the second, onomatopoeia. Both were so crowded at the start that students had to be selected on the basis of some claim of special knowledge. In Paradise, that year, we had one grandson of Oneida, one nun, one believer in the Skinner box, some students of Rousseau, the Constitution, Faust and Plato, and one participant in experiments with a new drug, psylocybin, under the guidance of Leary and Alpert, two young instructors in psychology. In Sound, I remember just one specialist, a pale, dark-haired Latin scholar, who rocked continuously in his chair whenever he read us onomato-poetic phrases he had found among the classics. The murmuring of innumerable bees in immemorial elms; l'insecte nette gratte la secheresse. Fairly late in the semester, when we were asked what our papers were going to be about, this young man said he wanted to write about the sound of corpses floating through literature. Oh, the professor said, with some enthusiasm, after just a moment's hesi-tation, you mean Ophelia. No, the young man replied, I want the sound of the sea.

To begin with, I almost went, instead, to Graham Island.

For a woman, it is always, don't you see, Scheherazade.

In nineteen sixty-four, the dean announced to the trustees that, for all intents and purposes—meetings, sleep, meals, electricity, de-mands upon her time and one another's—the students had abol-ished night.

"Brahms," he said, in explaining to a colleague why he did not attend that autumn's campus concert series. "All of it was Brahms. All, every. Eight. Things. Of Brahms."

Though he was my friend, I did not see Leander Dworkin often. We found that our friendship was safer on the telephone. Some-times we spoke daily. Sometimes we did not speak for a year or more. But the bond between us, I think, was less stormy, and in some ways more intense, than Leander's relations with people he actually saw. Once every few years, we would have dinner together, or a drink, or just a visit. Sometimes alone, more rarely with some-one with whom he was living and whom he wanted me to meet. One night, when we had gone, I think, off campus for hamburgers, I noticed, on Leander's wrist, several thin, brown, frayed and separating strands, like a tattered cuff of rope. Leander said it was an elephant-hair bracelet, and that Simon, his lover, had given it to him. It was frayed because he always forgot to remove it, as he ought to, before taking showers. Elephant hairs, it seems, are talismanic. It was going to bring him luck. Elephant-hair bracelets are expensive; they are paid for by the strand. In the following year,

Leander wrote many poems, and at last received his tenure. When we met again, months later, the frayed strands were gone. In their place was a thin, round, sturdy band of gold, which encased, Leander said, a single elephant hair. When I asked what had happened to the old bracelet, he said, "I lost it, I think. Or I threw it out." For some time, Leander had spoken, on the phone, of a woman, a painter, whom he had met, one afternoon, outside the gym, and whom he was trying to introduce, along with Simon, into his apartment and his life. The woman was in love with him, he said. She was married to a real-estate tycoon. Her name was Leonore. He was anxious for me to meet her. I knew that, in addition to his appetite for quarrels, Leander likes triads, complications, any variant of being paid for. But I looked at the bracelet, and I thought of Simon, and I thought, Leonore plays rough.

It was as boring, you know, as droning, and repetitive as a waltz, as a country-and-western lament in waltz time. It was as truly awful as a vin rosé.

Well, what did you pull out ahead of me on the road for, from a side street, when there were no other cars in sight behind me, if you were going to drive more slowly than I did?

It was early evening, in the city. The TV was on. We watched *The Newlywed Game*. The moderator had just asked the contestant, a young wife from Virginia, What is your husband's least favorite rodent? "His least favorite rodent," she replied, drawling serenely and without hesitation. "Oh, I think that would have to be the saxophone."

He knew that she had left him when she began to smoke again.

Is that where it begins?

I don't know. I don't know where it begins. It is where I am.

I know where you are. You are here. She had left him, then?

Years ago, he had smoked, but not when they met. So she stopped, as people do when they are in love. Take up cigarettes, or give them up, or change brands. As people do to be at one at least in this. Long after that, she began to smoke again.

So he knew she had left him?

Not knew, not left. Not right away, or just at first.

Why don't you begin then with at first?

Look, you can begin with at first, or it seems, or once upon a time.

Or in the city of P.

Or in the city of P. In the rain. But I can't. It is not what I know how to do.

Well, you must get these things straight, you know, resolve them in your mind before you write them down.

From the moment she knew that she was going to leave him, she started to look old. There was about her a sudden dimming, as in a bereavement or an illness, which in a way it was. He. They. Look, I would start short, if I could, with something shorter. The story of the boy, for instance, who did not cry wolf. Except that, of necessity, we can have no notion of that story, since the boy of course is dead.

So is the one who did cry wolf.

True, but he lasted longer.

Probably. I suppose that's right. He knew that she was going to leave him when she began to smoke again.

You can rely too much, my love, on the unspoken things. And the wry smile. I have that smile myself, and I've learned the silence, too, over the years. Along with your expressions, like No notion and Of necessity. What happens, though, when it is all unsaid, is that you wake up one morning, no, it's more like late one afternoon, and it's not just unsaid, it's gone. That's all. Just gone. I remember this word, that look, that small inflection, after all this time. I used to hold them, trust them, read them like a rune. Like a sign that there was a house, a billet, a civilization where we were. I look back and I think I was just there all alone. Collecting wisps and signs. Like a spinster who did know a young man once and who imagines ever since that she lost a fiancé in the war. Or an old fellow who, having spent months long ago in uniform at some dreary outpost nowhere near any country where there was a front, remembers buddies he never had, dying beside him in battles he was never in.

Hey, wait.

All right. There was, of course, a public world as well.

I was there, in Montgomery, Alabama, on a summer's day in

the late seventies, when the Attorney General of the United States, a Southerner himself, spoke at the ceremony in which a local judge, who had worked for more than twenty years, with courage and humanity and in virtual isolation, on the federal district court, was promoted to the Fifth Circuit Court of Appeals. That court, like the district court under the local judge, had been a great court, decent, honorable, articulate and brave. The Attorney General himself had, for some years, been a member of it—quite often, as it happened, in dissent. Here he was, though, in the late seventies, the Attorney General, Old Mushmouth, as the wife of one of the court's more distinguished judges had always, somewhat injudiciously and in his absence, called him, here he was, the Attorney General of the United States, speaking at the inauguration of a great federal district judge into a great federal appellate court. He mentioned the Ku Klux Klan. He alluded to it several times, the Klan. And each time, he referred to its membership, the members of the Klan, he called them. Clamsmen. No question about it, that's how he pronounced it. Clamsmen. It was no reflection on the Attorney General. True, the judge's wife had never thought much of his diction. True, in the court's most important decisions, he had been so often in dissent. But years had passed. He had come to speak well and to do honor. And this business of the Clamsmen, well, it may have had to do with molluscs, bivalves. Even crustaceans. I remember a young radical, in the sixties, denouncing her roommates as prawns of imperialism.

Alone. What an odd gloss we have here on Alone at last. Since alone at last, for every hero in a gothic, every villain in a melodrama, traditionally assumes a cast of two.
You know I hate wisecracks.
So do I.

One morning, in the early nineteen-eighties, Viola Teagarden filed a suit in a New York State court against Claudia Denneny for libel. Also named as defendants were a public television station and a talk-show host. Viola Teagarden's lawyer, Ezra Paris, had been, all his life, a civil libertarian; in every prior suit, he had been on the side of the right to speak, to print, to publish. He was em-

barrassed by *Teagarden* v. *Denneny* et al., which, as he knew, had
no legal merit. He justified it to himself on grounds, of which Viola
had persuaded him, that she was sad, hurt, pitiable, distraught. He
also thought, in friendship, that he owed her something. Her cur-
rent book was dedicated to him. But his province had always been
the First Amendment, and he preferred not to think about who was
paying his rather considerable legal fees, Martin Pix, a young, immensely rich, vaguely leftish media executive, who had recently
come, yacht and fortune, into Viola's special circle. That circle, as
I gradually came to understand, was one of the most important
cultural manifestations of its time.

Look here, you know, look here. All the things she had too
much class to mention were the things he never knew.
Well, but that's the point. I mean, it hardly takes much class
not to mention things if he already knows them anyway.

It was as though he had been born in the presence of the doubt,
the censor, the laugher at serious things, the unlaughing member
in the audience of a comedian, the voluble warner against places
where there is no danger, the reticent giver of directions toward a
place through which no one has safely passed. The check was forever less than half a step behind the impulse. Clamped to the hoof
of the Arabian horse of thought, report, or feeling, there were
always the teeth of the question: is this altogether true? The least
of the harm in it was the waste of energy and attention, in having
always to be doubly sure, in letting pass the moments of high possibility, in seldom taking action, in having always just a bit to under-
state and overprove.
Wait, wait, wait, wait. Can you not avoid, on the one hand,
the florid, overly elaborate, on the other hand, the arid exploration
of that after all limitless desert rock of desolation called Square One?
What are you, some sort of anti-claque?

Sometimes he loved her, sometimes he was just amused and
touched by the degree to which she loved him. Sometimes he was
bored by her love and felt it as a burden. Sometimes his sense of
himself was enhanced, sometimes diminished by it. But he had

come to take the extent of her love as given, and, as such, he lost interest in it. She may have given him this certainty too early, and not just out of genuine attachment. One falls out of gradations of love and despair, after all, every few days, or months, or minutes. With courtesy, then, and also for the sake, for the sake of the long rhythms, she kept the façade in place and steady, unaffected by every nuance of caring and not caring. He distrusted her sometimes, but on the wrong grounds. He thought of her as light with the truth, and lawless. And she, who was not in other ways dishonest, who was in fact honorable in his ways and in others, was perhaps dishonest in this: that not to risk losing him, or for whatever other reason, she concealed, no, she did not insist that he see, certain important facets of her nature. She pretended, though with her particular form of nervous energy she was not always able to pretend this, that she was more content than she was, that her love for him was more constant than, within the limits that he set, it could be.

Well, he came to see me one night when he was drunk, bringing his dog and walking with his flashlight. We gave the dog some water, and I drove them home. He did that on several nights, over the years. Usually I heard footsteps, outside on the path, and the metallic collar of the dog.

She was going to leave him, she thought, on or about their thirty-fifth anniversary. Or, rather, his.

Bartok was what he played, Bartok and Telemann. But what moved him was Wasting Away Again in Margaritaville. What lifted his spirits one season was I've Got a Pair of Brand New Roller Skates, You've Got a Brand New Key.

When we had been in graduate school, in Cambridge, for just one year, Maggie, a friend from college, announced that she was quitting, moving elsewhere, moving on. I asked why. After all, Maggie, I said, this is Harvard, Cambridge. It's been only a year, here we are, just two semesters. Why? "Well," she said, "I've played this card now."

This is the whole hand, so far as I know it, not played out entirely, of course. But the bridge, baccarat, double solitaire, twenty-one, old maid, hearts, blackjack, fifty-two pickup. Obviously poker. I've played this card now.

What do you tell the Sanger people? Lily asked. In those days, the only people who made love were these: in the colleges, stringy-haired, lonely daughters of left-wing urban parents; in the high schools, pretty girls who got pregnant and got married; in the adult world, women who, in typing, teaching, theater, publishing, art, were stymied in their jobs. The men who made love to the left-wing college girls were either medical students, who had contempt for them and forgot them, or jocks, who bragged falsely of having made conquests of quite other girls. The boys who made love to the high school girls were football stars, who settled down to families. The men who made love to women in the adult world were married men. Most children outside marriage, in those days, were conceived in drive-ins or in cars parked on country roads near reservoirs or other quiet places. The pill may have altered this pattern less radically than the proliferation, not just in sports cars but in all cars, of the bucket seat. Homosexuals may have made love in those days, but it was almost universally believed that the world included five, or at most nine, homosexuals. Brothers and sisters may have made love, but that would not have been widely known. As for married couples, there seemed to come to them, quite soon, a bitterness. What I'm trying to say is that sex among young people in those days was rare.

When you marry, the great Spanish scholar said to his seminar, late one afternoon in spring, make sure your lives are different enough so that you have something to tell each other in the evening. Maybe he was tired of being told things. Make a joke of it, perhaps, or an epigram. But not every time, for God's sake, not every time.

Here's what seemed to us, in those days, at a major college, with serious feminist traditions, a daring story with an important dénouement. The two professors were legendary, Dr. Vickers, Miss Collins. They had refused to marry, in the early nineteen-twenties, when the president of the college had insisted that they must. They had been anarchists, living together in a cottage some miles from the campus. Anarchists with principle. Anarchists with tenure. Anarchists in love. There was no certainty that the college president, or even the entire faculty, could dismiss them. The issues were profound: traditions of the community of scholars and independence; traditions of *in loco parentis* and the middle class. One evening, in the second autumn of this quiet scandal, the college president drove her Packard to the cottage. An early suffragette and a lifelong spinster, she spoke to them by their first names. Rufus, she said, Amanda, this cannot go on. Certain standards must prevail. She asked them, for God's sake, for her sake, for all their sakes, to marry. Dr. Vickers asked her to sit down, and told her that they had in fact been married since last May. The three old friends had sherry and got drunk together. But for all time, from the twenties onward, the couple, both historians, were known as Dr. Vickers and Miss Collins, and treated as unmarried, as though their respectability were an embarrassing secret, and their intractability of many years a source of pride.

One morning in the late fifties, Bonnie Stone, an academically and socially ambitious senior from New York, who often overslept, or overate, or overdressed, but who relied in crisis on a certain flirting charm, was late for an appointment with Dr. Vickers. In fact, it seemed she might have missed it altogether. They stood, that afternoon, in the library corridor outside his office. Bonnie was explaining, loudly, volubly, elaborately, with an expression of perhaps too intense apology. "Don't worry, sweetie," the old professor said at last. "I've been stood up by better-looking broads than you." Apart from a remark by a lecturer, untenured, concerning speculation about Byron and his sister—a remark so daring in its cavalierness and obscenity that no two versions agreed as to exactly what it was—"Don't worry, sweetie. I've been stood up by better-looking broads than you," were the most shocking sentences, within the academic setting, that any of us had ever heard.

The world is everything that is the case.
And in the second place because.

Did I throw the most important thing perhaps, by accident, away?

Here's how I know that I've already lost him. Jake is driving. I am in mid-sentence, or mid-anecdote, or halfway through a question. Though it's neither the hour nor the half hour, he flips on the radio news. I know I've lost him then, because I have. And yet, at five on a cold and snowy morning, Jake had picked me up for the long drive to the city. Cars were few. It was still dark. With the radio on, he talked. He pointed to a place where, he said, on the road to my house, he had seen two deer. That was all he said. A few nights later, we went to a party, at about an hour's distance from our town. Jake and his wife had picked me up for the drive there. His idea. I have my own car. Late that night, on the road back, he said, "Honey, right there in that heavy snowstorm, I saw two deer." There was a silence. I thought, he calls her honey. I could not imagine what his wife thought, or why she said nothing, or why the silence seemed so long and deep. His words were clearly not addressed to me. He had already told me about the deer. He has never called me anything but Kate. Then it dawned on me. He had told his wife, too, and forgotten that he'd told her. She must have thought he was telling me for the first time, and that, whatever honey has come to mean between them, he now calls me that. I could be wrong, of course. She may not even have been listening, or maybe she never answers at that hour. There we both were, though, together in our silence. There he was, a little drunk, unaware, I think, and happy, driving through the darkness down the road.

Crying was not, was by no means, her modus operandi. Nonetheless, she wept.

In the sixth year, I went to New Orleans by myself.

How could I know that every time you had a choice you would choose the other thing?

This is about the wildlife commissioner. And the houseguest, an animal. Henry James would have known what to do with him.

Flannery O'Connor would have dealt with him in her way. New England environmentalist writers would have wrung from him whatever can be wrung from the birth of their meaningful foals in darks hours or from symbolic encroachments by highways on family meadows. For Conrad, perhaps, it might have been a man. But it was not a man, this creature with which I had a misunderstanding. It wandered, late one afternoon in winter, into the small room, almost a closet, which contained a stove, in the old barn where I used to live. The weather was grey, a few snowflakes fell. It was very cold. I sat in a shabby armchair, reading. I felt watched. When I looked up, I saw the animal, with delicate paws, a sharp face, and high, arched fluffy tail, sitting up, staring at me, through the open doorway, from a place beside the stove. A moment later, he vanished. I thought I might have imagined him. After a while, I went to look. There was some reddish fluff, in a narrow gap between the insulation and the wall. I had switched on a small lightbulb, which hung from the ceiling. I left it on, then closed and, to my surprise and half-smilingly, locked the door between that room and my own. I did not fall asleep until very late.

In winter, not wanting to slide the large barn doors open, I used to enter and leave through the back door of the little stove room. When I left, early the next morning, the creature was not there. I was not sure what he was. I was still not entirely sure I had seen him. I did not turn off the lightbulb. I spent most of that day in the city. When I came home, long after dark, it was snowing, and he was there—sitting, this time, on the stove, slouched and leaning against the stovepipe, head lowered, great, dark-circled eyes blinking, swaying a little, I thought, like a drunk. He left through his crawl space almost as soon as he saw me. But because, on every subsequent evening, he stayed longer and left less abruptly; because he returned most nights, and slouched, on the stove, leaning against the stovepipe, all night, until morning; because he sometimes touched, though rarely, the water I left in a dish beside the stove for him; because he was, after all, a wild thing, growing ever more docile; we arrived at our misunderstanding. I thought he was growing to trust me, when in fact he was dying. So are we all, of course. But we do not normally mistake progressions of weakness, the loss of the simple capacity to escape, for the onset of love.

And the virtuoso, and the pachysandra, and the awful night of Eva dancing?

Not right here, I think. Not now.

I thought he was growing to trust me, when in fact he was dying. I had hardly an intimation of this until one night when, as usual by then, the light in the stove room was on, the door was open, and I again sat in that armchair, reading. About the third time I looked up, the animal, which had until then slouched, staring, blinking, against the stovepipe, was evidently trying to climb from the stove down to the floor. I thought at first he was trying to reach the water dish, or that, startled by my looking up, he was going to leave through the gap between the insulation and the wall. But, as he stayed there, head and front paws reaching, slowly, tentatively, toward the floor, his haunches, most of his weight still on the stove; as it seemed that gravity had somehow reversed for him, and that the simple act of getting down required all his strength, had become a slope too steep for him to climb; I began to walk toward him, intending, at that moment, just to lift him to the floor. He looked at me. I reconsidered. I moved quietly to the phone book and the phone. When I had finished dialing, a very young voice answered. "May I speak to Doctor Rubin?" I asked, meaning Ed, who had treated all our dogs and cats since I was in kindergarten; Ed, who had put his hand to the side of his face and said, "Oy vey geschrien, oy vey geschrien," when my mother brought in Shaggy, the wonderful mongrel hit by a speeding pickup; Ed Rubin, who had let us stay with Bayard, our always slow-witted and timorous but now senile Great Dane, while he gave him the shot that put him gently away; Ed Rubin, whom I'd last seen with his wife, Dottie, who always used to sing so lustily in the choir, not just of the local synagogue but of various other congregations, blinking, as the lights went up, at an improbable French movie in New York. "This is Doctor Rubin," the young voice replied.

"Wayne, this is Kate Ennis," I said. I had read to Wayne Rubin when he was five. "I'm living in a barn on King Street. There's a raccoon here, and I think he's sick. Could you come? He's just trying to lower himself from my stove onto the floor, and he can't seem to make it. I think I'm going to try to lift him down."

"Don't touch him," Wayne said. "Don't go near him. There've been a lot of sick raccoons around since fall. It's distemper."

"Well, what shall I do, then?"

"Don't touch him, Kate. Don't go near him. Just stay out of his reach until he dies. Where did you say he was?"

"He's here in the barn, with me. On the stove. He's been warming himself here for days. Would you just come and have a look at him?"

"I can't. Not tonight, Kate. But here's what you do. Call the wildlife commissioner. He'll help you out."

"Will he come?"

"Yes, he will. That's his job. Look him up, in the phone book. Under Township of Red Hill. Wildlife Commissioner."

"Thanks. Wayne, how's your father?"

"He's fine. He and Mom are in Fort Lauderdale till March."

"I see. Well, thanks."

"Right. And, Kate, don't go near an animal with distemper. Or any sick, undomesticated animal. You know that."

I did know.

About an hour after my call, an old battered panel truck came into the driveway. I was waiting outside by then, partly from impatience, partly because the barn was not easy to find, partly to stop standing and watching the by now obviously feverish and exhausted creature, which had somehow raised its whole body onto the stove again, and sat up, precariously, leaning against the stovepipe, blinking. The night was very cold, windy. A grizzled old man, in a patched woolen jacket and an old cap with earmuffs, climbed slowly out of the truck. Out of the passenger side, equally slowly, similarly dressed, climbed a boy of about ten. I said, Hello, I'm Kate Ennis. "Well, ma'am, I'm the wildlife commissioner. And this is my grandson." I mentioned the lateness of the hour. "That's all right, ma'am. The family was watching the TV, but this is my job. And the boy likes to come. We'll just take care of this for you real nice." The man fumbled for a time in the rear of the truck, then brought out a large dented cage, made of barbed wire and wood, and a long wooden pole, with a loop of leather at one end. He handed the cage to the boy, kept the pole for himself.

"Well, ma'am," he said, "where is he?"

"He's inside. On the stove. I was wondering. What are you going to do with him exactly?" Something flickered in the man's face: one of those. For the first time, he looked directly at me, from head to foot, then, for a moment, in the eyes.

"Why, ma'am, we'll just take care of him for you," he said.

The boy was already walking toward the barn. I opened the door for them. We approached the stove. The boy moved forward, crouched, then made a purring sound, and slid open a panel of the cage. The raccoon just sat there, shivered, stared.

"See his hindquarters," the boy said. "Paralyzed."

The old man, standing in the doorway, said nothing, wheezed, then, not at all quickly, moved his pole, thrust the loop over the animal's head, and, lifting him by the neck, let him dangle a moment, then dropped him into the boy's cage. The boy slammed the panel shut. The raccoon turned around, stared out. "He's very sick, ma'am, didn't even fight me. Usually they do," the old man said. The boy stood, blank-faced, purring. "Give him penicillin. That's the best thing for him," the man continued.

"Look," I said. "I know he's dying. What I meant was, do you shoot him, or give him gas, or just leave him alone and let him die?"

"Oh, no, ma'am," he said, looking me up and down again, this time more slowly. "Penicillin. Then I'll see if he'll just eat for me. If I can just get them to eat for me, I know I can fix them. But don't you worry. He'll die humanely." He laughed. The boy stopped purring. Holding the cage, he started toward the truck.

Outside, I asked the old man how much I owed him.

"Well, ma'am, I work for the town," he said. "Whatever you think is appropriate." He put the bill in the pocket of his shirt, inside the jacket. The raccoon looked out through his cage, in the back of the truck, beside some rags, an inner tube, some lengths of pipe. The boy sat quietly in his seat. The old man got in, and they drove away.

God knows what they did with him. Stoned him, probably. Unless raccoon pelts had value, more value than acts of cruelty, in their lives, in which case they would probably waste a single bullet on him, or let him starve. Maybe this isn't about the wildlife commissioner. About betrayal, rather, on my part. Or on the animal's, reproach. He did trust me, after all, in some sense, or was entrusted to me. We traveled a bit along life's road together; at the time he came to visit, I even, as I rarely do, had my own few days of fever. But in making more frightening and miserable, probably, the last moments of this raccoon, well, I made an error. I should have let him die, of course, upon the stove. A mistake, a series of errors, first of love, then of officiousness, finally of language. I should have known, I ought to have known, but how could I? what is meant by, what are the official duties of the wildlife commissioner in this town.

Long after I wrote to London Exit, I heard from Los Angeles Hemlock.

Yet here I am, after all, alone at last on Orcas Island.

Be the first on your block to, what? Come out of the closet. Make a breakthrough in medicine. Go to West Point. Sell to a black family. Enlist in, or resign from the avant garde.

We have the sins of silence here. Also the sins of loquacity and glibness. We have the sins of moderation, and also of excess. We have our sinner gluttons, and our sinner anorectics. We have the sins of going first, and of After you, Alphonse. We have the sins of impatience, and of patience. Of doing nothing, and of taking action. Of spontaneity and calculation. Of indecision, and of sitting in judgment on one's peers. We try to be alert here for infractions, and when we find none, we know we have fallen among the sins of oversight, or else of smugness. We have the sins of disobedience, and of just following orders. Of gravity and levity, of complacency, anxiety, indifference, obsession, interest. We have the sins of insincerity, and of telling unwelcome truths. We have the sins of ingratitude for our many blessings, and of taking joy in any moment of our lives. We have the sins of skepticism, and belief. Of promptness, and of being late. Of hopelessness, and of expecting anything. Of failing to think of the starving children in India, of dwelling on thoughts about those children, of failing to see the relevance of another spoonful to the situation of those starving children, or to Uncle Bill, or Granny, or poor Joel, or whomever we are being asked to take another spoonful for. We have the sins of depression, and of being comforted. Of ignorance, and being well-informed. Of carelessness, and of exactitude. Of leading, following, opposing, taking no part in. Very few of us, it seems fair to say, are morally at ease.

I'll get over it.
Will you?
Yes. I just don't understand it. I guess I will never understand it. We've done the Blue Angel, somehow, in reverse. No, I don't mean that. Nothing here, though, of frolic and detour, nothing of calm and beauty, where I might have joined you for a moment, or a weekend, or a night. You didn't want it.
But I did.
Maybe we better start again.

At the time, we had a Secretary of State who was always saying hogwash. Hogwash, he would say when it was rumored that there were tensions between his own staff and another. Hogwash, that there was an Arabist tilt in the foreign service. Hogwash, that we would send military equipment to defend some vital interest somewhere in the world. Our chief negotiator for disarmament, at that time, thought that tensions in the world could be most productively discussed in terms of apes. "Apes on a Treadmill" was, in fact, the title of a piece he published in a respected journal of foreign policy. It was his earnest thesis that the relation between the great powers was, profoundly and in essence, monkey see, monkey do. Both these men had been in public life, in various capacities, for a long time. Both were lawyers and, when they served in government, gave up enormous private incomes. It seemed odd to me at the time, perhaps it was an Ivy League or legal scruple, or, since doctors and nurses had it too, a Hippocratic inhibition, or, since no one in the country or even in the world seemed to disagree, a universal scruple or perhaps a failure of imagination; in any event, it seemed odd to me that no one, in those early days, no statesman, diplomat, doctor, nurse, friend or enemy, wife for

God's sake, seemed to contemplate, in the night, a simple, gentle
act of euthanasia for the Shah.

What do you tell the Sanger people? Lily asked.

You are, you know, you were the nearest thing to a real story
to happen in my life.

Would it have cost him all the earth, sometime in all those
years, to take her to New Orleans for a week?

Look, the sun is a sort of bribe, you know, and so is a heavy
thunderstorm or a snowfall. So is a dawn, though not I think a
sunset. So is a warm bath or a shower, and a sound sleep. Bribes all,
in the conspiracy of everything to continue to exist.

You've left out the B Minor Mass, Mozart, all kinds of music.
Also pleasure in high speeds, the deeply comic, something to eat
or drink, success in an enterprise.

Well, all of them have their ingredient of death, you know.

And you've left out love.

So I have, so I have.

"You owe me ten dollars, Leander Dworkin!" the blond young
man was screaming, late at night, on the sidewalk on upper Broadway. That was in summer, the early sixties. Leander wanted no
one to know he was gay, thought no one but the men he slept
with, whom he always swore to secrecy, did know. How they hated
him, those men in their Village duplexes, or on the beaches of
Fire Island, for his insistence, for this particular form of the pre-
tense. It mattered bitterly to them, the *way*, by the morning after,
he denied them. But Leander insisted, and thought he could en-
force the demand, that they keep his secret. Of course, they did not.
And then, on that summer night almost twenty years ago, on account of his unwillingness to honor debts, his liking to be paid for,
even his taste for threesomes, he found himself, after midnight,
virtually running along a sidewalk on upper Broadway, pretending
to ignore Simon, his principal lover, Simon whose feelings he had
hurt even then by inviting Howard, whom he had met at the gym,
to move into their apartment, Simon, to whom he owed debts of

various kinds and who was now running in the dark beside him, screaming for all the world to hear, "Leander Dworkin, you owe me ten dollars! Ten dollars, Leander Dworkin! You owe them to me!"

Let me just say this about Homer. That part in the Odyssey, about the weaving and the unweaving, and the suitors. It cannot be true, not quite that way, and Homer, I think, never meant us to believe it. At home, the faithful wife, with their son, Telemachus. Weaving. On the road, Ulysses, fighting, all those years. Fighting, as it happens, to bring another man's woman, Helen, back from Troy. But that is not the point. The point is that, through all the years Ulysses was away, doing battle in the Iliad, traveling and having adventures in the Odyssey, through all the years of the war and his return, his wife was faithfully at home. Weaving. Surrounded by suitors, it is true, but she explains the matter, or Homer does on her behalf, in this way: that she rejected the suitors, kept them all at bay, by constant daylight weaving, and the claim that she must refuse them all, until her work, this carpet, or blanket, or tapestry perhaps, in any event this piece of weaving, was complete. Then, at night, every night, she secretly unwove what she had woven by day. Unobservant, for some time, these suitors. Unobservant, too, Telemachus, a troubled child. It is hard to know, at this remove, whether the underlying situation was simply a conspiracy among the wife and suitors to conceal that she had been sleeping with one, or maybe all, of them. It is only clear that, as a faithful wife, she had two difficult circumstances to explain. The presence of the suitors, and how very little weaving she had done. Enraptured as he always was with cleverness, Ulysses believed the story. Or pretended to. After all, he slew the suitors all the same. But that his wife did not unweave by night, and therefore by implication hardly ever wove by day, we've known ever since we learned, not what love is, but what reporting is and what public figures are, and how much more than we were ever taught to expect is really lies.

What I wish I had not lost is the photograph of him, the only nice one. What I wish I had not lost is the ticket for my raincoat at the shoe repair shop. What I wish I had not lost is the suitcase with the letters. What I wish I had not lost is the time, or the inventory of the lost things, or the consciousness of all the things that are not lost. But nothing I had, I think, is anything Jake's wife wants or ever wanted. Nothing was lost, I think, by any of us there.

What do you tell the Sanger people? Lily asked.

Let me just mention people's expression when they are bored by a confidence, or when their minds are elsewhere, or when they have been told it once already. Let me mention, too, a confidence of long ago, an intimacy, completely, as it turns, out, misunderstood.

A rowboat, without oars. An outboard motor. As you can sit there for years, forever, with that outboard motor, pulling again, and yet again, that rope, or cord, or wire, or whatever it is, and winding yet again, and each time, every single time, the motor, though it may give a cough or two, will fail to start, though if it starts, and when it starts, you are, at whatever speed you choose, within the engine's limits and the hazards of the course, well on your way, *until* it starts you are no nearer where you were going on the fifteenth try than on the first; the enterprise may last forever, and yet never quite begin. The fact seems to be, however, that unless some apparently unrelated event should intervene—a bullet, a heart attack, a loss of interest, a cry from shore that dinner's ready, or company has come, or junior's run away—the engine will eventually start. In the meantime, though, while you have been intensely busy, it is difficult to account for how the time is spent.

What do you tell the Sanger people? Lily asked, late one afternoon in those years. We were well educated, certainly. We had read widely. And there was no "we," of course, except in retrospect, since it's just an I, alone, who reads. We had, all the same, failures of information. The books which determined to such a large extent what we would become were, well, sure, Beatrix Potter, *Little Women*, Dickens, war and frontier novels, Albert Payson Terhune dog books, Kipling; then, suddenly, poetry, great classics, any or all of them, Dostoevski, Conrad, Melville. With a transcendent, though far from complete comprehension. Hemingway, Salinger, Fitzgerald; then lastly, oddly, in some ways pre-eminently, John O'Hara.

How could he have known that? He could not possibly have known
it. For some, at an impressionable age, Ayn Rand. Also, inevitably,
mountains of trash. *The Amboy Dukes*, for instance, forbidden in
all schools and read by everybody. Forget it. Don't think about it.
There were the other interdicted books, *God's Little Acre*, even
Sanctuary; but we didn't understand them. We may have read and
reread, with curiosity, D. H. Lawrence. But if we were, in the end,
as young adults and in sexual matters, anybody's creatures, we
were also, though we would never have mentioned it to one another, John O'Hara's. Highly educated. Even original or finely
tuned. But his creatures all the same.

That year, finally, in those years, we knew it was absurd. We
had been adamant about how our lives would be, not like the
stereotype daughters of left-wing urban parents, not like the fallen
woman in all of letters, not even like the adulterous women in
O'Hara. So few of us anyway were married, as his women seemed
to be. But, apart from everything else, we were beginning to sense
in ourselves the creation, if not of another stereotype, at least of
another predictable pattern. Unmarried. Waiting. Studiously cooking dinners. Going out. Working, on that carpet, or blanket, or
tapestry perhaps, in any event, that piece of weaving. Keeping
alive the sense of high romantic possibility. That possibility which,
educated and even worldly though we were, we knew, from all of
letters and from our generational respect for institutions, was a
matter of not going to bed with people unless you were going to
marry them. That year, finally, it became absurd. What do I have
this apartment for, Maggie said, after a few months of her first job
in the city, if I'm never going to sleep with anybody in it? We were
drinking gin. We had been talking about people it seemed we were
not going to marry. Confronted, then, with a lack of information,
we remembered Margaret Sanger. So we took out the phone book,
and found what turned out to be the Sanger Institute. At that moment, at that very moment, the phone rang. It was Lily, and she
said, What do you tell the Sanger people? But she was not that
close a friend, and she was younger than we were. So Maggie replied in a way that, though worldly enough, was noncommittal.
Anyway, we didn't *know* what you told the Sanger people.

The next morning, Maggie called them to arrange for an appointment. And they asked her when she was getting married. Maggie paused. Then, with great presence of mind I thought, she said December ninth. And they said, they honestly really said this, that they were sorry but they didn't make appointments earlier than five weeks before a wedding day. Maggie said, I see. Two hours later, she called and, not thinking she could use her own name again, made an appointment in my name. The next day, in a seizure of cowardice or paranoia, I called the Sanger Institute. The voice I reached had a German accent. I thought, oh my God, I know these refugee voices, this person is probably some immigrant doctor's wife, some friend even of my own parents. So I didn't cancel the appointment, or say anything at all. Since I hadn't can- celed, though, I felt obliged to go. When I got to the waiting room, there were so few people, nobody looked like me, my courage failed. I left. I called Maggie from a phone booth and we met for coffee. So that we were only able, after all, to inform Lily that what you told the Sanger people was that you were getting married in five weeks.

Twenty years later, I again spoke to the Sanger people. I was looking for a worthy, touching charity to receive a check on my behalf. The check was in settlement of my own suit for libel. Noth- ing like *Teagarden* v. *Denneny*. Libel actions, I knew, had always been one of the real slums of Anglo-Saxon law. From Oscar Wilde through Alger Hiss, they seemed almost always grim, misguided, profoundly tainted, in some way, at the source. The grounds for my own suit, however, against a rich sensational publication, had occurred to me, one afternoon, in a state of high hilarity, as the first sound and witty libel suit of which I had ever heard. I thought it only required just the right charitable beneficiary for a check in settlement.

Worthy, the Sanger people. Maybe. But touching?

Well, I know. I was looking for a home for babies, unwed mothers. Something on that order. I even called the Foundling Hos- pital, which I'd walked by a hundred times, and asked them if they really were for foundlings. They said, Yes, but please hold, Sister Elizabeth would discuss it with me. And I thought, I can't, in view of the present state of things having to do with abortion and birth control, send this check to a Roman Catholic institution. I called the Sanger people, and I said, I can't tell you why, but I need a worthy, touching charity to have a check sent to. What is it exactly, apart from Planned Parenthood, that you do? And the voice said, Well, abortions. I said I didn't think that was what I had in mind. She said, If you came down here, you would see some very touching, moving abortion cases. I said, I know, I know, but what is required in this case is something more like babies, foundlings, a home for unwed mothers. She said, Well, we have our fertility institute. And we do have a place for unwed mothers. I said fine. Worthy and touching. And they got their check.

Is he not going to call, then? I don't know. I guess he's not. I seem to be having a harder time with this than I thought or it was worth.

In France, they have the story of a ballet dancer so moved by her role that, in a scene in which she was supposed to be dying, and touchingly reunited with her mother, she actually blurted Maman, and her career was ruined. It seems you have to keep, you just have to keep a distance.

I wonder whether he will ever ask himself, say to himself, Well, she wasn't asking all the earth, why did I let her go?

Here's how it is now, at the women's college, which is still scholarly, still feminist. There has been a compromise with the nearest all male college, which had threatened, otherwise, to go co-ed. Ten percent of the male students now live at the women's college. Ten percent of the female students live at the men's college. Since some of the feminist dormitories have chosen to admit males, while others have chosen not to, the campus is now divided into two groups, which refer to each other, solely on the basis of the single-sex or co-ed dormitory issue, as the lesbians and the whores. The antipathy between the groups is deep. Students are "coming out" as lesbians, who, in the old days, would have been thought of as shy, or bold, or having crushes, or simply loyal in their friendships, but who would not have been, probably are not now, lesbians at all. And students are declaring themselves whores as though that were the only heterosexual choice. The dean's office believes that to the degree that it still has responsibilities *in loco parentis* it ought not to act but just sympathetically abide, providing a benign place for things to sort themselves out. The latest, now, is this: whores and lesbians have found an issue on which they are united, unanimous in fact. The issue involves shower curtains at the gym. Male gyms do not have shower curtains. Male athletes are not hidden in the showers from one another. As a symptom, a residue of shame about the female body, the shower curtains, the students say, as with one voice, must be removed.

Those of us who remembered how relatively worried for our privacy we were, in those years, suspected campus-wide intimidation. Those of us who are of an age to be trustees, and to have young daughters, and those daughters timid, asked the most timid daughters what they thought of the shower-curtain crisis. And with one voice, though their mothers asked them separately, they said: Remove the shower curtains. So that's what we'll do. And, whatever may become of the declared whores and lesbians, what will happen if someday, somewhere, they are asked, Are you now or have you ever been one or the other, about the shower curtains, and that unforced unanimity, well, we know it's fine.

Baby's all right, Uncle Jacques and Aunt Zabeth used to say in times of worry or of crisis. Baby's all right. A friend of theirs, an only child, had always said it, like a little incantation, when he was alone in the dark and frightened, from his babyhood, through his childhood, all his life. His friends took it up. Think of the RAF, my mother would say, for the same reason, at such times. Think of the RAF. Baby's all right.

The world is everything that is the case. And in the second place because. In the sixth year, I went to New Orleans by myself. Look, I can't. The relation between storytelling and eroticism is always close. I mean, it's not just a matter of spinning yarns.

Yes it is. Spinning yarns.

Not any more, I think. Not even in thrillers, which is the path the purest storytelling impulse took. Not even in thrillers. Where stories are, there is always sex, and sometimes mortal danger.

You mean in stories.

I mean in telling them. Sex, mortal danger, and sometimes reprieve. For a woman, it is always, don't you see, Scheherazade. For a man, it may be the Virginian. There he goes, then, striding through the dust of midday toward his confrontation. Here I am, of an evening, wondering whether I can hold his interest yet a while.

Did I throw the most important thing, by accident, away?

There was this about the infestation. First, the tent caterpillars, clustered black in grey-white webs at the clefts where trunk and branch, twigs and branches met, loathsome gossamer, sticking to hands, eyebrows, hair, as one tried with a broom or a branch to disengage them, everywhere, filmy, hopeless, travesty of silk. Sprayed them. Blasted them with torches. Must have missed a few or, more likely, they came again, borne by the wind. The crab apple was bare of leaves. The birches dangled leaves half-eaten, covered now with creatures advancing by hump and stretch, never seen to eat, only seen to crawl and rest, leaving devastation, overnight. Then, new buds, new leaves, a second growth. Within days more, the gypsy moths. Little beige egg casings all over the bark of every tree; hanging from stringy webs, at the same time, capsules, lacquered, layered, like some strange dessert, eggs in the cases, caterpillars in the hanging pupae, powdered wings on the night air, so prolific an infestation that we had three simultaneous generations of gypsy moths. They ate nothing, of course, that summer, just left their progeny to sleep and wait, on virtually every surface, on the fence, the firewood, the wisteria, webs, adobe casings, pupae, waiting all winter as we brought in and burned the firewood, sleeping, repellent, waiting, just as we waited, I suppose, for spring.

And if I had a complaint about the matter, it was only this: that you did not help me with it. Not that you needed to help me, not that I even needed help. In the end, I called the agriculture station, and they told me what to do. But the point is that, at the time, your land, your many acres of trees were being sprayed against infestation. And when I asked you the name of the people who were spraying your land, so that they might spray my acre and a half as well, you said you could not remember their name. Then, I asked where I ought to look in the yellow pages, and you said, and I'm afraid you said this with some small satisfaction, that it was probably in any event too late to look, because the infestation this year had been so widespread and intense that all professional sprayers would by this time be booked up. Can this be as I am telling it? That was certainly not, at the time, how I perceived it, though I know that at the time I felt dimly, more than dimly but for obscure reasons, sad. And when the builders came to make the addition, the huge addition to your new house, with much digging, and blasting, and refilling, and moving of the earth, and you praised, rather daily praised, the young Irish contractor in charge, and I asked whether he might know someone who, when his job with you was done, could dredge the silt that has accumulated in my pond, you said, No, you thought the job too small for him. Months later, when you praised and praised two brothers, Finns, who had come with their backhoe to dredge for some source of water at your place, and I asked whether they might have or know someone who had a backhoe for my pond, you said you had forgotten their names as well, and they were gone. I thought for a time this was on your part some fastidiousness, some discretion, in not wanting to have the same workmen engaged at your house as at mine. Weeks later, though, you had no hesitation in asking Paul and his son, while they were working on my land and on my time, whether and under what circumstances they might come to cut, and split, and stack your firewood. You had asked me for Paul's name, and I had given it, but you talked with him at my place. You did not call him at home.

It may still all be all right. I think I have found someone to spray my trees, and even someone to dredge the pond. All last night, an immense backhoe at rest towered over my house, and this morning it is at work, ringing and thundering out there. The contractor is unknown. I mean, no one around here seems to know him. It may all be more expensive than it might have been. That is, when the kind old professor came to visit, and suggested that, since I would have anyway to dredge the silt, I might as well at the same time construct a little island in the pond, he also said to be sure to have a man arrange things, because contractors are somehow disinclined to work as well or as honestly for women as for men; and when I told you what he had said, you agreed that it was so. After the dredging is done, I suppose, the place will really look much better, and the danger of floods will have abated. But I guess I also know that the time has come, and that I ought to sell my house. And there it is. Because if these were not failures of love, on your part or on mine, or failures of generosity, or at least of imagination or attention, well, of course, they were, and I didn't want to know. And though I know my heart cannot have been broken in these things, these things of my house and of yours, no, it can't have been, I'm sure it was not, I find that I am crying as I write, because, it cannot either, can it? have cost so much to say in some of these things, or in some others sometime, not grudgingly, and without reluctance, Yes.

Look here.
I know.
Would it have cost him all the earth, sometime in all those years, to take her to New Orleans for a week?

The world is everything that is the case. And in the second place because. And in the second place because is how the Nabokov story starts, and I hate the artifice, but it is a star turn. I mean, what a star turn, what a triple coup to begin a story thus, with "And," when nothing at all has gone before, with "in the second place," when there has been no first place, with "because," when there has been no why and there will be no indication *what*, what thing, what happening, what act, what state of mind, will follow on account of that because. The world is everything that is the case, of course, begins the work of Wittgenstein, and more. So dry and flat, in its self-contained, almost impacted quality there is nonetheless a kind of rolling thunder. True, self-evident, beyond any *doubt*, it creates a terrible sense of what it is possible, what it might be worthwhile, to say at all. Language, thought, advancing like bulldozers, like cement. *Die Welt Ist Alles, Was Der Fall Ist.* Who could argue that the world includes things that are not the case, that some things that are not the case at all are hidden somewhere in the world? Only a specious poet or a trendy French philosopher, toying with metaphor, unworthy of the statement's august truth. And yet, after the first flash of awe and admiration, the loss is inescapable. I mean, who wants to write specious half-truths. On the other hand, who wants to write cement.

The townhouse twins played the purest countertenor, on the stereo, also Germaine Montero singing Spanish folksongs. Men who sing like women, the super said, bewildered, and women who sing like men.

Here's how it is in the city, on our street. For the eight years since I moved into this brownstone, they have been building a branch of the subway, to some obscure, unnecessary destination, no one seems to know exactly where. The project has meant, at least, those years of jobs for hardhats and of extra business for the deli. Hardly any inconvenience, apart from diminished parking spaces taken up by the large green structures in which the hardhats eat their donuts and drink beer. Hardly any noise, at least on our street. In deference to the block associations, which are strong here, the city agreed to muffle the nightly whistling and blasting, also, an expensive concession in this line of work, to save the trees. Inside, the first two floors are occupied by the landlady, one or both of whose late husbands must have said that what they loved about her was her temper. From time to time, she needs to throw an all-night party, with singing from *The Fireside Book*; at other times, though, far more frequently, she needs to provoke quarrels, pound on a tenant's door, and scream. The house only has four floors. When I'm in town, I'm the tenant on the third floor, just above our landlady's duplex. Brian and Paula, both young lawyers, both the first in their families to go beyond high school, are on the top floor, with Apple, their Afghan hound.

In the winter, right after New Year's, our landlady likes to take a cruise around the world. She sublets her two floors for six months and goes. Whoever moves in then inevitably changes the character of the house to some degree. Last year, we had a banker and his family, who were the children and grandchildren of a war criminal. This year, all day on weekends and sometimes after school on weekdays, a child comes and endlessly picks out "Frère Jacques" on the piano. Pausing, hesitating, never getting it quite right, using sometimes one hand, sometimes two, alternating, though this month is March, with a few notes from "Jingle Bells." One night, when Brian went to look for something in the basement, he encountered an armed man, whom he took to be a prowler. The man was a bodyguard. The family in our landlady's duplex this year, it turns out, lives under a pseudonym. Their real name is Somoza. Today, this morning, someone is using a hammer and a blowtorch on a house across the garden. Apple has begun to bark. And Madame Somoza cowers behind her shades and draperies at this quantity of noise.

Very amusing, the rich Italians always say now when they're here. Or else, Not very amusing.

By the time the old couple moved to the suburbs, she had become flatly, almost by reflex, ornery. He was a sort of engine of cliché. "Rome wasn't built in a day," he might say, over his brandy. And she would reply, without hesitation, "Yes it was."

Maybe he won't be there when I get back. Maybe I won't either. Who would have thought that every time he had a choice he would choose the other thing.

Did it mean nothing, then, that he came to see her every day?

Oh, it meant a lot, a lot. And I don't hold with saying, at every mood and moment, This is how I feel, this is what's happening now to me. I know reticence has its depths. I really do. But you can go too far with the undone and the unspoken things. What it comes to in the end is that there's only an ambiguous footprint, a hair that could be anyone's, a drunken moment that I couldn't actually swear to, though it held me for a few years longer, to say that there was ever a living creature there. And while I was moved to tears when you walked here in the night, with your flashlight and your dog—not to tears, I guess, but to a stillness of the heart—it was really with your dog that you walked in the moonlight and the woods, and I drove you home. A man I know used to speak of women as high or low maintenance. Since his world was city life, what he meant was that one kind of mistress requires furs, cars, constant small attentions; another kind asks much less. I guess I've been high maintenance in just this sense: that you've given me more time, on those rides, business travels, visits in the interstices of your life, than you ever planned to give. What you've done, though, is to arrange your life so that all the things with a little joy or beauty in them were the things in which I had no part. No, I don't mean that. It is only that I didn't think I set the price so very high. There wasn't ever going to be a price. Yet here I am, after all, alone on Orcas Island. And it's just that what happens now is just so bleak and ordinary, either way.

Hey wait.
Well, love after all is a habit like any other.
A habit, maybe. Like any other, no.

Drivers of large cars drive extremely badly. So do old men; men wearing hats; men with thick necks and florid faces; hunters; drivers of cars with dented fenders, or with more than one generation in them, or with college stickers on their rearview windows, or with slogans on their bumpers, or with license plates of names or words instead of numbers, or with New Jersey license plates. I have left out matrons, nuns, dyed blondes, old women; their lapses tend to be blunt and unaggressive, like an inability to park or a wrong turn on a one-way street. That is all I know, categorically and without reservation, about drivers. Two other facts I think I know are these. Nobody ever confides a secret to one person only. No one destroys all copies of a document. Also, that it is children really, perhaps because so much is forbidden to them, who understand from within the nature of crime.

You are, you know, you were the nearest thing to a real story to happen in my life.

Yet here I am, for the first time and yet again, alone at last on Orcas Island.

Did I throw the most important thing perhaps, by accident, away?

Having read in the paper that a London society called Exit was about to publish a book of pharmacological instructions for terminally ill people who simply wanted to die, peacefully, in their sleep, I thought of Ed Rubin and old Bayard. Then, I misplaced the clipping and forgot. Months later, when I found the clipping and remembered, I wrote to London Exit. Nothing happened. No reply. Long after that, when I had again forgotten, I received a letter from a Los Angeles society called Hemlock, who said that, since I was an American, London Exit had forwarded my communication to them. I had a moment of hilarity about this. The clear sense of jurisdiction. Then, I read, in a newsletter enclosed by Hemlock, that London Exit had never published its instructions. They had been enjoined from publication, and suppressed. Exit's officials, moreover, had been indicted under the English law of suicide, aiding and abetting. Los Angeles Hemlock, however, was going to go ahead and publish. I called and asked how they were going to keep from being suppressed under the California equivalent of the English statute. Their plan, they said, was to publish, not instructions, but short case histories: Harry, weighing this many pounds, took this many grams of this substance, and it wasn't enough; Anna, who weighed less, took this many grams more, and it was. No law could prevent the publication of case histories. Not when we have the protection of the First Amendment. That was that. Hemlock published. There was, though, this improbable footnote from London: Exit, it seemed, may really have aided and abetted, even proselytized. Witnesses were coming forward to say that, in response to their phone calls of the most tentative inquiry, a voice would offer to come at once. Within hours, an elderly man would appear on their doorsteps, offering to help, urging them to be spared further misery, from their asthma, their sadness, their lower back pain. Another moment of hilarity. And yet. And then it passed.

The lines, as usual, were long and extremely slow going into the island's airport. Immigration officials considered each passport with an impassive but somehow insulting deliberateness. It was also possible, given the quality of local schooling, that they found it difficult to read. Lines for departure from the island were also, equally, slow, but they had about them always something of the frantic. Reservations, clearly marked on tickets and many times confirmed, were somehow missing from passenger lists; or even if they appeared on the lists, where passengers, reading upside down, could clearly see them, the airline employee would look up, with that impassivity, that insulting deliberation, and repeat that there was no record of the passenger's name, that the passenger could wait, if he liked, on standby, for this flight or for the next in six hours' time. It hardly mattered which island it was. Barbados. St. Thomas. Tortola. Martinique. Visitors, particularly those who most deplored the quality of island food, liked to say the French islands were different. But they were not. With the exception of Jamaica and Grenada, where violence was overt, the islands were the same.

What you found in all these places was, of course, the clear, warm sea, the sun, the long white beaches; and, in the water, always in recent years, at least one young, possibly feeble-minded black person, smiling, playing with himself. Nearby, a large, loud transistor, a group of young blacks, some in bathing suits, a few in trousers, chattering in the island patois, moving gradually nearer a sunbathing young white woman, or a sunbathing white couple, until that woman or that couple, whose intention had evidently been to stay at some distance from the others, picked up their towels and moved toward the groups around the beach umbrellas, where the other white people were. Elsewhere on the beach, not all day but inevitably by noon, a second group of blacks, young, laughing, wading deep, splashing, shouting, embracing, taunting, concealing in a kind of ostentatious, faked exuberance, the fact, true of so many places with sought-after resorts, sought-after beaches, that no native islanders knew how to swim. These were the tensions of arriving, staying, leaving. On the heavily frequented islands, where people went for nightclubs, gambling, golf, hotels. And on the remote, secluded islands of rented and guarded houses. Where people came to be undisturbed. And then became restless after dinner.

Look here.
How could I know that every time you had a chance to choose you would choose the other thing?

Do you know, he said, I have not made love with anyone since I first made love with you. I said, Not anyone? He said no. I said, Neither have I. And there we were. And why is it not enough, for people of diffidence, hesitation and reserve, to let it go, to let it be now, this way, for the rest of our lives? Well, perhaps I am wrong now. But every once in a while since the year we met, no, not met, since we didn't for so long even like each other, since the year, then, that we began to go to bed together, I said that someday, in spring or autumn, I'd like to go to New Orleans. I had never been there. And you said, each time you said, Why I'll take you there, that's easy. In the sixth year, in August, I went to New Orleans by myself. It was all right, though it was hot, since it was August. I just hadn't thought it through. I invented errands, talked to those judges, spent a few days. It didn't matter. Then, from time to time, I began to say, You know, someday we ought to go somewhere for a weekend. Not for work, as when we fly to Cleveland, Chicago, or Atlanta, and we have an early dinner there or else I wait at the motel while you have dinner with the local people, and the next day I read while you do the work you came for, and the next night, or two nights later, we fly back. But a weekend of calm, as though you were in your houses, on your islands, your long walks. Sometimes, you said, I will, we'll do that. Once or twice, you said, We'll see. It became a sort of joke between us, that weekend. Sometimes it was reduced to just dinner at a restaurant in Pennsylvania, not far from the place where you sometimes spend a few days fishing; but we never went there, either. Other dinners, not that one. And it began to matter. I don't know why. A child's thing. On the other hand, I'm not sure you can say, as a not inconsiderable man to a grown woman, We'll see.
And then one night, when you were about to leave for the

island where you spend your weeks at Christmas, and your wife was already there but your children, the last of whom has now grown up, were not this year going with you, I said, I'm afraid I said, You know, we wouldn't have to make love as much as this in a night, in a single night after a day of tiredness and errands, and before an early morning of more errands and long absence, we wouldn't have to make love as much as this in a single night if someday we had a week. It was late. We were drunk, though not very. And then I said, You know. You said, What. I said, I guess we are never going to have a week. And then I'm afraid I wept. We were quiet then, as we usually are. But there are things you can say, I think, or suggest, or even contemplate aloud just once. And I had begun. So I said, because after all these years I had to say something, though it may be far too late to say it, When it's time for me to go, do you want me to ask you or tell you or should I just quietly go. You said, But I don't want you to go, I need you here. I said, No, and in a way you've wanted me to go for years, and I've known it, but I just couldn't do it. Then you said, not speaking as to a child any longer, But you can't go, everything will just disintegrate if you go. I was touched, and I said whatever I said, about how bored you are sometimes. You said, But you always have something new to tell me; and if you go I'll just shrivel up, I'll just shrivel up like a prune. We went to sleep. And by morning, of course, you had forgotten. Remembered by afternoon, I think, only that I had been unhappy, remembered a phrase or two, but remembered by then as though it were a childhood thing, one of your daughters homesick at school, perhaps, or briefly sentimental at parting when you and their mother went away, or, more recently, when they went away themselves, to their men or their jobs, abroad. So it was only as if I had said once again that while you were gone I would miss you. And we have said that so often, everyone says it, in such a formula way, it has almost no meaning. And to make me feel better, you said again that you loved me, and gave me, as a sort of Christmas present, that word about your having made love only with me in all these years. And I could not, how could I, turn away, so I just said, Not anyone? and then, Neither have I.

We had drinks and dinner early, because you had to get home, after your tiring day, in time to be picked up for your morning flight. And we talked, as we do, of the news, and our errands, and maybe something comic in them. Then, since I couldn't stay with you, or you with me, on account of the driver in the morning, you took me home, and I gave you a chicken liver for your dog and a pill for the night, and you gave me some letters to mail. After which, I'm afraid, I cried again. You seemed bewildered by that. I said, You know, the thing is you build your life a bit. And you said, The thing is it's built. After midnight, and this is very unusual for us, you called and said you loved me, and I said whatever I said, also Catch a lot of fish on your island, and that I would see you when you got back.

I only don't know if I will see you when you get back. That is all that is wrong, or some of what's wrong. That I shouldn't be here when you get back, that I ought not to have been here many times before, that I know and knew that with anything I have of instinct or of wisdom. The Germans say no one can jump over his own shadow, and I used to rationalize, no, not rationalize, think, that I couldn't ask you to jump outside your *way*. But what I'm afraid I've done is lost, lost you something, lost me something, lost us, by what I did not insist, a possibility. Because there is no reason in the world why, in eight years, we have never had, and we will never have, a week. And because I am not one of your daughters, nor one of your assistants, nor your wife, nor a dependent friend or colleague, nor a litigant clamoring for your attention, nor a politician who seeks your advice. Or even, as I once said, in the dark, with a smile, a secretary or a blonde in a chorus line with whom you are having an affair. You said you wouldn't be having an affair with either of the last two, but the truth is, we would probably be better off if you were. If I were that secretary or that blonde, though as you say your life is built, you would have to find room, make some kind of room. The weeks on the north island in summer, the other island in winter, the hunting and walking weekends, even the occasional junket to the Riviera or to London. Somehow not with me, not with me. Not Christmas, of course, or birthdays, which I know don't really matter. I just don't know quite how I let it happen. Perhaps I had no choice, or perhaps you never loved me quite enough, and I didn't want to know.

So here we are. Or rather, there you are and here I am. And

maybe the thing is simply not to think about it, and grow old, older still, like this. What we have now, it is true, is that you come to see me almost every day, and you bolt your morning tea, or your evening Scotch, and when I said the phrase that occurred to me, for the first time, to characterize the way you sometimes leave as Making good your escape, you did laugh. And you often spend the nights. But I may as well confess that, though I love you and seeing you changes the character of my mood and day, I sometimes dread, I don't know how else to put it, sometimes dread a kind of visit that you make to me. I long for you to be here, miss you when you are gone, but sometimes to wonder whether I can amuse you, or whether you will be bored, tired, called away for bridge, or work, or tennis, or because one of your daughters has had a whim, well, sometimes I dread what will follow such a visit, and so I've come to dread a bit the visit, too. And while that may be true of any couple, any marriage, we have reversed it somehow. In the scheme of things, the mistress has something of the island; some of the strain, routine, and sense of long, cold winter belongs with the wife.

When you are away, there are these traces: a few notes left on my front door, saying you'll be late or asking where I am; a French pocket knife with a single all-purpose blade; two Liberty scarves bought with leftover currency at foreign airports; and, of course, the passage of the years, and the location of my house. You've moved the whole arsenal of the Other Woman, somehow, into your own house, and at my place, when you come, there's only me. I wonder if you know at all what is happening in my heart, what a word. I suppose you don't. You've so many females, wife, sisters, daughters, cousins, dog, in your life that you've probably confused me with them all. I guess I like to think that you love me more than you know, though I suppose the grounds are pretty slim for saying that. Well, a child's thing. But you are, you know, you were, the nearest thing to a real story to happen in my life. Also, look at it this way, just what is it that I, that we are going to have, to look forward to, to look back on, after all. I mean, here I am, for the first time and yet again, alone at last on Orcas Island. What are you going to do? What you've always done, I guess. But what am I going to do, what shall I do, now?

"I'll get over it."

"Will you?"

"Yes. And you'll find somebody else." Your face froze. You said, "I won't." I said, "You will. The thing is, I won't mind so much. Because I won't know."

Look here, you know. I loved you.

Well, the question occurs, so many times, clearing desks, doing income tax, looking for letters, documents, some are missing, one doesn't know for sure which are lost, doesn't dare even to look too carefully, time and time again, there is this, Did I throw the most important thing perhaps, by accident, away?

II. PITCH DARK

Quanta, Amy said, on the train, in that blizzard, in answer to my question, Quanta.

Not here, Diana said, to her lasting regret, to her own daughter, who approached her, crying, in front of all those people. Not here.

Just ax for José, the young man said, on the ride out to Newark Airport. You need a ambulance, or a driver for any reason, you call the same number. Just ax for José. Also, when the People Express terminal loomed nearby, just beyond the small maze of side streets and overpasses: You can see it from here; but just try to get to it.

Quanta. Not here. Just ax for José.

You are very busy. I am very busy. We at this rest home, this switchboard, this courthouse, this race track, this theater, this nightclub, this classroom, this office, this lighthouse, this studio, are all extremely busy. So there is this pressure now, on every sentence, not just to say what it has to say, but to justify its claim upon our time.

So the sentences leap, do they? on stage, do all the business for which they have been so long in training, then go, panting and gagging, offstage until they are called again from the wings. Is that what you mean?

MINDFUL, no, but mindful, as they say at the start of every paragraph of every mindless, interminable, often simultaneously bland and vicious UN resolution, Mindful of these pressures, I ask you all the same to trust me, stay with me here a moment, I'm alone.

"Now these," she said, "are from Isfahan. And these are from Chichicastenango." She was old. She had been, for more than thirty years, beginning at the time and with the help of Senator Joseph McCarthy, the dragon of the passport office. Now she was retired, showing me her house. "When were you in Chichicastenango?" I asked, holding my little notebook. "I don't recall the year," she said.

To begin with, I almost went instead to Graham Island.

I broke the law, perhaps I ought to confess this at the start, I fell afoul of the law at last, in an unlikely place, on the road to Dublin from a town called Cihrbradàn. I left at three in the night, unseen, I hoped, unheard. I was saved, further down the road, by a teamster to whom I lied, though he did not ask me much, and who may have lied to me as well. A lorry driver, they would have called him there, but his truck was immense; he drove, as he told me, all night two nights a week. When I asked, he said he was a union man, so he would have been a teamster here. I left the country and the jurisdiction by plane and traveling under a pseudonym, or a name that was anyway false. I am a fugitive from the jurisdiction now. But then, in extenuation, there were so many things. In extenuation, there are always so many things. The surgery. My state of mind. The shady business at the airline ticket office. Look here, you know, look here. I am trying to leave. All the little steps and phases and maneuvers, stratagems, of trying to leave him now, without breaking my own heart, or maybe his, or scaring myself to death, or bounding back.

This is the age of crime.

Was there something I did, you think, or might have done, I ask you that, some thing I did not do, and might have done, that would have kept you with me yet a while?

This is the age of crime. I'm sure we all grant that. It's the age, of course, of other things as well. Of the great chance, for instance, and the loss of faith, of the bureaucrat, and of technology. But from the highest public matters to the smallest private acts, the mugger, the embezzler, the burglar, the perjurer, tax chiseler, killer, gang enforcer, the plumber, party chairman, salesman, curator, car or TV repairman, officials of the union, officials of the corporation, the archbishop, the numbers runner, the delinquent, the police; from the alley to the statehouse, behind the darkened window or the desk; this is the age of crime. And recently, I think the truth is this, over a period of days and nights some weeks ago, I became part of it. How else account for the fact that I found myself, at three a.m. on a dark November night, haring in a rented car through the Irish countryside, under a sickle moon? At times it rained. Sometimes the sky was black and clear, with the moon and stars precise and perfect overhead. It was cold. The car's radiator did not work. And there I was, speeding along the road, I hoped, toward Dublin, from a place called Cihrbradàn. I had no clear plan, but I thought I had at most ten hours to be gone.

Beside the road, invisible, the fields, the long stone walls. On the road, few cars, three perhaps an hour, all of them coming toward me. Nobody following, then, no one in pursuit. And yet, as I passed through the small, dark, widely separated towns, I wondered whether my headlights and engine were noticed, whether a policeman, perhaps, or some sleepy but eager informer, had picked up the receiver, and called the next town. Phones ringing, then from town to town, not even for me necessarily. What lawful errand, after all, could send a cheap, small rented car out on a Southern Irish road, at this speed, in this weather, at this hour? Except that, with any luck, it no longer gave much sign of being a rented car. That afternoon, in broad daylight, I had peeled its rental sticker off. In fact, though I did not know at what precise moment I had crossed over into crime, that removal must have marked a turning point. On the one hand, they, they could say that it proved guilt or at least criminal intent. I, on the other hand, I could make what I had begun to think of as the argument of What kind of fool do you take me for. I mean, do you take me for such a fool as to remove a rental sticker in broad daylight when what I have in mind is a furtive escape. The argument, I knew, hardly ever worked, in politics, or criminal law, or private life—and yet, in my case there was no criminal record, and so little evidence. It made no *sense* for me to be doing what I seemed to be doing, in view of what little I had done. I might prevail. Sleet came down. It was pitch dark. Rarely, every twenty or thirty miles, there was a light, a single lighted window, in a house. With, behind it, a poet, a wakeful mother, a worker on the night shift, a terrorist, with a clock, and caps, and fuse? What I had felt for days was fear. Alternating with a sort of double suspicion: that the fear was groundless. Now, as the sky became clear again, I felt what every vandal must feel as he races through the night: dawning exhilaration. Out there, Orion, darkness, the incredible unseen beauty of the Irish countryside. If not real joy, at least a waning trepidation. Then, within an hour, I had reason to think I had missed my turnoff at Castlebar.

I stopped. I pulled over on the left. Driving on the left had been so much of the problem until then. I got out and, in the dark, under the headlights, I looked at a map of Ireland. There was no sign, no mention whatever, of a tiny intersection I had just passed. The words on the roadside marker, R.9 Lockarnagh, did not appear on the map at all. But I concluded, from the time passed and the mileage, that I had, in fact, missed the turnoff. So I turned, and raced back in the direction I had been coming from. A car, now, coming toward me, lowered his headlights and went by. But I could not make out his license plates, or even the color or contours of his car. I had to assume he could not make mine out, either. He had arrived too late to see me stop and turn around. If he had been following me, then, he was going the wrong way. Miles passed, more miles. The road no longer looked familiar. What were the odds, I thought, what were the odds that my mother's daughter, the descendant of my ancestors, should be lost like this, late one night in Ireland, fearing what was after all the law, under this sickle moon? Well, I'd been with Yemenite servants and the wives

of nuclear physicists in a bomb shelter in Rehovoth, with Ibo tribes-
men at a military installation in a nameless town. As much as this
is the age of crime, after all, this is the century of dislocation. Not
just for journalists or refugees; for everyone. I was by no means the
first in my family to have reason to fear the law of a nation, or to
seek furtively to escape from its jurisdiction and its police. But it
was cold. I was alone, and it was dark. I thought I was lost, and
then I looked at my gas gauge. A quarter of a tank. I would have to
look out for gas stations, not that I recalled having passed any that
were open. On the highway to Dublin, surely, there would be one.
If I could find the highway. Headlights appeared in my rearview
mirror, distant at first, and then closer. I pulled over to the left, off
the road again, got out and flagged down what turned out to be an
enormous truck. I'm sorry, I said, I seem to be lost. Could you tell
me how I get on N.5 to Dublin. He hesitated. A shifty, wily look
of suspicion, which I thought I'd seen innumerable times since I
arrived in this strange country, passed over his face. Then he said,
I'm going to Dublin. You can follow me. He drove off, and I followed. What was that look of suspicion, I wondered, could he have
taken this nightrider who flagged him down for a terrorist? Why
not. Who else would be out, at this hour, flagging people down?
Then I wondered what load he was transporting in that immense
truck. Come to think of it, I had seen no other trucks on the road
that night since Cihrbradàn, certainly none of that size and weight.
Could he be carrying gelignite, at this hour? Was he, perhaps, a
terrorist, and did that look of suspicion cross his face because he
feared for a moment that I was the police? Strange odds, those, too,
for my ancestors.

But there we were, he and I, haring single file through the
Southern Irish countryside. I was no longer alone. A new fear, a
sort of paranoia, crossed my mind: had he hesitated because he
planned to mislead me, was he heading, not toward Dublin at all
but straight back to that place named, come to think of it, like some
hybrid out of Freud and Kafka, Castlebar? Miles and miles. No
signs that I could see. Irish road signs, in any case, are grey-black
on grey-white, and in print so small that they are virtually illegible
to any driver on the road. From time to time, I kept looking at my

gas gauge. Then, I sped past him, drove, slowed, stopped, switched on my hazard lights and stood in the road to flag him down again. Patience, no look at all of What is it this time? on his face. I said I was running out of gas. I secretly hoped he had some, but I did not mention it. Is there likely to be a gas station pretty soon? I asked. Not till nine-thirty in the morning, he said. How much gas did you have when you started out? Three-quarters full, I said. Well, then you ought to be all right, he said. Of course, like so many things that were said to me in Ireland, this seemed to make no sense. I mean, surely it depended, not on how much gas I had when I set out, but on how much would be required for the distance that remained, or at least how much I had where I was starting *from*.

Maybe what we have here is Mayerling for one. Maybe Mayerling always was for one.

There we stood, though, this tall broad man and I, in the sleet, on the road, in the beam of his enormous headlights. I asked how much farther it was to Dublin. He said, About a hundred twenty miles. Are there no all-night gas stations in Ireland? I asked. He said no. Well, then I guess I won't make it, I said. My flight from Dublin leaves at ten. A pause. We stand, not looking at each other. The sleet has abated. His headlights are muted now, and diffused by mist. Do you suppose, I ask, speaking as slowly as the thought evolves, that I could drive till I run out of fuel, and then ride the rest of the way with you? He reflects. He looks toward his truck. He seems less surprised by the question than I am. That would be all right, he says. I ask, Where shall I leave my car, at some closed gas station, or just any place where it runs down. Oh, he says, locked, I think, on the street at Ballyhairness. I find it difficult to understand what he says, not just because he speaks softly and I am unfamiliar with his accent, but because, as I now notice, he has a stammer. In any event, I have grown by now to love him. I wonder whether he is going to leave me after all. But as we drive, miles and miles, at speed, the sky is sometimes black, with that clear moon and stars, sometimes mauve, sometimes filled with rain;

though my gas gauge has gone well beyond the red and rests firmly now on empty; though I have no clear plan, and I'm in my way alone again; in due course, a sign appears. What it says is Ballyhaunis 10. And though I have a moment of freefall panic, what if he doesn't stop? on the whole I trust him now, and what I think is, Well met, teamster.

The truth was, there was something in the ice cube.

The turning point at the paper was the introduction of the byline.

Here's who I knew in those days: everyone.

Everyone?

Well, not everyone in the world, of course. But a surprising number and variety, considering the lonely soul I was when I was young, and the sort of recluse I have since become.

"It's really too much. I can't tell you who they'll seat next to you," Claire said, after dinner, at the guarded island villa. "Wives, Canadians. They sit you next to anyone." Also, "The daughter married an octoroon. A baboon. I don't know."

It began at the airline ticket counter. No, it began with another lorry driver, three days earlier, at midday, in a small town, on the road from Shannon. No, with the fact that we were brought up to be honest, or the fact that my parents fled. Well, wherever it began, the ambassador, a great and kind man, in his youth a poet and a war hero, now a banker and owner of vast farms in Iowa, had offered me his house, a castle really, empty now but for its little staff, on the Irish coast at Cihrbradàn. In his absence, the house, the grounds, the staff, especially, were forlorn. Talk to them, he said, as he spoke of Celia, Paddy, Pat, and Kathleen. They are lonely and a friendly people. Celia, the cook, missed having guests at table, and preparing picnics for them. Paddy missed shooting parties. Ask Paddy where to shoot, if shooting was what I wanted. Otherwise, ask him where to go for walks. Talk to them. Stay all of November if I liked. The offer was not only kind; it seemed providential. I am a reader of horoscopes in tabloids. Even at the best of times, I look for portents. Within hours, I had set out, standby, on a crowded flight to London. All night over the Atlantic, beside me, a coughing man, evidently feverish. In the morning, at Heathrow, the shady business at the airline ticket counter. But, when I got to Shannon, and had crossed the tarmac in the rain to a dim hangar marked Baggage Claim, I thought, Well, at least, at last I have done something. I have come this far. I found a booth, and a pale operator, who put me through to Cihrbradàn. I asked Paddy for directions; he said, just follow the signs, it is all quite clearly marked. I passed down a long corridor, through customs, and entered the airport itself. The stalls for the car-rental agencies were lined up in a row. It was like a Levantine bazaar, a bazaar in Baghdad, Cairo, or Damascus. The men in the stalls were shouting, hawking, gesticulating, hissing at me, psst, psst, as though I were a cat, or (but this is another story) a woman who has inadvertently wandered, in Manhattan, into the wrong room of the Century Club. For some reason, I was apparently the only likely customer. The other passengers had already left, or were walking with a clearer sense of destination. I stood, hesitant, at some distance from the stalls. The wheedling and hectoring so surprised me that I headed toward the exit, and the taxi stand. I reconsidered. I approached the youngest man in the row of stalls, a frail dark-haired fellow of about eighteen. How much would it cost, I asked, to rent his smallest car for about a week. He named a sum. I paused. He cut the price by nine dollars a day. I said all right. But then he both miscomputed the amount and drew up the sum in Irish pounds instead of dollars. When I mentioned it, he tore up the form and began again, with an air of exasperation and absent-mindedness, as though he had never done anything so practical as to rent a car before. There's no charge for mileage, he said. He crossed out Mileage, and wrote in Fuel: $35, and added a line: Misc. Tax: $19. Finally, he asked whether I would like insurance. I wavered. My sense of the transaction somehow gave me no confidence in the quality, or even the fact of this insurance. I said, No, thank you, I am insured. Why, so are we, he said. This is just for the initial liability, eight hundred dollars. I would normally take this kind of insurance without question, but there was something makeshift about even the piece of paper, which he now held out to me as if it were a raffle ticket; and, in fact, I was insured, as a driver, for major accidents. So I signed the waiver of insurance, and the contract for the rental of the car.

Talk to them, the ambassador had said, they are a friendly people. Well, the hell they are. An occasional creature of great poetry and beauty; the others, suspicious, crafty, greedy, stubborn, incurious, stupid, devious, violent, and cruel. And, of course, that is what the history of the country is. Point, set, and match, as the American professor's wife said, at dinner, at the Waltons', on the night I concluded that I had to leave the country. On the night I drove and drove, and became ever more certain that I had missed my turnoff, in which case I was bound, not for Dublin at all, but for Tuam and for Shannon; or perhaps worse, lost entirely. So that I would drive, through this alternating sleet and mauve and breathless clarity till daylight, calling attention to myself at daylight, when what I needed was to catch the first flight of the morning out of Dublin. A flight on which I had no reservation, but on which I had been told, in response to an anonymous call the night before, there were still seats. Then, when I had stopped and turned around, there were those headlights coming toward me, the first car I had seen in more than twenty minutes; and I thought, Could the police have alerted one another, in every little town along the way, ever since I set out from the castle, dropping my key in the intense dark at Cihrbradàn, and could this be another of their agents, sent to follow me out of the station at Castlebar? Not so paranoid a thought as that, for many reasons; not least, because the police in this country must be accustomed to following nightriders of all descriptions, Protestants, Catholics, gunrunners, suppliers, enemies, members, betrayers of the IRA. And then, of course, I was following my teamster. But what grounds to trust him, after all? In extenuation; but why raise so defensively this matter of extenuation, since, so far, I have done nothing; I have only come this far.

"My dear," the English publisher said, "we were in their dining room, looking out on their balcony, and the skyline of Beirut. With each course, the talk became more gruesome. 'Tell them, Mina,' the brother would say, 'in what condition they left your fiancé, that night, on your doorstep. And about the note they enclosed, in the small box, with his hand.' 'Ah, but I will tell also,' the girl would answer, 'in what manner, and how quickly, we exacted our revenge.' Mind you, we were eating. I looked at them, and I thought, This is la crème. La crème de la crème de la Phalange."

The airport, I notice, is absolutely silent. A carnival silence, of crooks, muggers, embezzlers, swindlers, terrorists, thugs, burglars, traitors, swindlers, rapists, but here I am on shaky ground. This is the age of crime, but it is not yet at this moment that I begin to be in the shade or the shadow of the wrong. I pick up my bags. The frail dark-haired man, key in hand, and carrying an umbrella, accompanies me out into the rain, and across the parking lot, to a small yellow car, with a slightly dented door. It is true that he is talking amiably, about the weather, about the route, but I am still carrying my bags. Finally, he opens the car door for me, says, Safe journey then, and walks away. Well, the car's radio doesn't work, nor does the heater; and I misunderstand, it turns out, the windshield wiper, which flaps (as I drive, I count) only once every thirteen seconds. Bidden or unbidden; that is, whether the switch is on or off. The road signs, virtually indistinguishable in this weather from the color of the sky, often do not mention even the largest towns. Galway, for instance, is sometimes mentioned, sometimes not. The car-rental man, like Paddy, said to follow the signs for Westport. But there are no signs for Westport. I do not look at the map of Ireland, which lies folded on the seat beside me, because, in the intervals between those desultory, spastic, and somehow each time startling flaps of the windshield wiper, the windows are completely misted over. For some reason, I am also disinclined to stop. The car-rental man also said that the distance from Shannon to Cihrbradàn was about thirty miles, but I've already driven more than sixty. I begin to persuade myself that what the car registers is kilometers. I have heard and read so much, through the years, about Galway, however. I know there will be, there is sooner or later bound to be a large, clear sign for Galway. Finally, I pull over to a large gas station, and wait beside the fuel pumps. Nobody stirs. I walk through the rain toward the office. A pudgy young man, with sandy hair and freckled lips, is standing just inside the door. I say, Could you tell me, please, am I still on the right road, and

how far is it, to Galway? He stares off into the distance. I stand
there in the rain. Then, looking me straight in the eyes, he says,
with unmistakable satisfaction: I've no idea. He watches as I get
back in my car, and set off, on the same road, in the same direction.
I try the radio and the heater again. Nothing. A silence and a chill.
Of the three forward speeds on the floorshift, I now notice, one is
only intermittent; on even the smallest hills it does not always hold.
I wish I had thought to ask him which was the nearest town. I
have just about decided that I am in fact off course, so far off, and
so long ago, that the man had looked, not sullenly pleased, but just
bewildered, never having heard perhaps of Galway. Within half a
mile of that gas station, there is a large sign: Galway 6. Well, maybe
he didn't like me, or understand my accent. Maybe he's never
traveled as far as six miles from where we stood, and the sign is so
familiar to him he forgot. Maybe he has a mother, or an older sister,
who likes to look at him blankly and say, in that tone of voice: I've
no idea. Whatever it is, the rain stops, and the road is right. Still
bemused, but taking heart, I drive.

I enter a small town; and, as I round a curve, on the cobbled
road, I hear and slightly feel a sort of crack, or smack, on my side
of the car. I think I've grazed a truck, a very large truck, parked
half on the sidewalk, half in the road, along that curve. I get out
and, to my great relief, I find that I have only hit his bumper. Or
rather, his front bumper, being high off the curb, has hooked under
my left front fender, just above the hubcap, tearing that fender in a
straight line, from the rim behind the tire to the door hinge, a
distance of about a foot. The fender, oddly, is not bent, only cut in
that straight, tidy line. The edge of the truck's bumper, on the other
hand, heavy steel covered in thick rubber, is bent very slightly forward. That is all. A young man walks across the street. I say, I've
hit your truck. He says, I guess you have. When he sees what has
happened, he is at first as relieved as I am. He says, Fortunately,
there's no harm, fortunately; and starts to bend his bumper back.
Then he sees the rental agency's sticker on the rear window of my
car. His eyes narrow, and he says, Is that a rental car? I say it is.
He says, very slowly, Rental cars have insurance, and asks to see my
insurance form. I say I haven't one, just the rental agreement, and
start to look for it in my purse. Still trusting, I say, I guess I ought

to see your driver's license then, we ought to exchange them. He says, There's no need. It's nothing. Fortunately there's no harm, fortunately. He looks at my car, says, I just don't want them coming after me. I find the rental agreement. He takes it, says, I'll just be a minute, show this to the agent, for his advice. Then, he walks rapidly away.

Time passes. I don't know where he has gone. By agent, for some reason, I think he meant a news agent, and from his allusion to advice, I assume the news agent is some sort of worldly friend. More time. He does not return. I park my car in a better spot, further from the curve. The town, it occurs to me, is absolutely still. I look for the news dealer, find him, ask where the truck driver might have gone. The man is oddly evasive at first, seems to know nothing about the truck, the driver, or the events, for that matter, which have just taken place, in that stillness, on a curve just a few yards from his door. He waits. Suddenly, he says, Perhaps he's gone to the police station. I ask where that is. And though the street is the only one in town, and though it has on each side at most ten small buildings, either he, and the other people in his shop, and two people I subsequently ask are incapable of giving directions, or I am too rattled and obtuse to follow them, but I cannot find the police station. More time. I walk more slowly. I notice a doorway over which there is a small blue porcelain medallion, lettered, perhaps in Gaelic. The windows are dark. The door is locked; it has no handle; and when I knock there's no reply. Twenty more minutes. I've walked the length of the town, several times, returning always to the truck. I wonder how I'm going to manage without my rental agreement, but I give up. I start to walk, again, toward my car, when the truck driver comes out of I don't know which door. Where have you been? I ask, in an almost apologetic voice. He says, I've been to the agent, for his advice, it's all taken care of, there's no harm done. Although, for some reason, I still don't altogether distrust him, I say, You know, I'll need that rental agreement back. He's been walking toward his truck. He says, It's all right, I believe the agent has it. And his eyes shift briefly, involuntarily, toward the doorway under the medallion. The door is now slightly open. I walk toward it. The driver turns to follow me, runs. We enter almost at the same moment.

At the right of the room, which is small and almost completely dark, sits a policeman, writing, by the light of a small lamp, in a huge, lined ledger, at a wooden desk. The back of the room is dark, with, darker still, in outline, what appear to be three chairs. At no moment so far, not at the airport, not when I thought I was lost, not even when I heard the slap of bumper and fender, or in the long wait since, have I felt the slightest rush of adrenaline. Now, for some reason, I'm a little out of breath. The policeman says, It's all right, ma'am, it's taken care of. I say, almost accustomed now to not understanding and feeling somehow remiss, Well, officer, how do you mean? He is wearing his helmet, and writing in his ledger. He says, We've already rung the rental agency, and they have said they'll pay. I say, No, don't you see, I didn't sign for their insurance. Under the agreement, I'm the one who has to pay. The policeman continues writing, says, It's all right, ma'am, I've spoken to them, and I'm nearly finished. I say, Well, in that case, don't you see, officer, I'll need your name, and the driver's, and a copy of your report. It's all right, ma'am, the policeman says, I've nearly finished it. I say, But you haven't seen my car or even the truck. He does not reply. I say, Surely you're going to come and see the truck. As though this were a new thought to him, he gets up reluctantly from behind the desk. His helmet has been on the whole time. And I am still, or again, deluded, perhaps because they both seem so slow and unintelligent, with a kind of idiot trust. At the door, the driver, perhaps by now embarrassed, says, The damage of course is nothing. I just didn't want them coming after me about your car. In this matter of the commas. In this matter of the paragraphs. In this matter of the scandal at the tennis courts. Not right here, I think, not now.

We walk to the truck. When the policeman finally sees, after I've pointed it out to him, that the bumper is bent, he starts to press his own foot against it, pauses, steps back, says to the driver, I guess you'll want to bend that back. The driver, sensing perhaps a loss of allegiance, looks at us both and says, very slowly, I'll want to get an estimate. The policeman, as though recollecting himself, says, He'll want to get an estimate. I say, Look, since I'm responsible, why don't we go together for an estimate, and I'll just pay. Silence. The driver says, Oh, I can't go now. I ask when he might be able to go. He looks away and says he can't say at the moment. Beginning at last to get an intimation, I say, Why don't you simply tell me your own estimate of the damages, and perhaps I could pay it to you now. He hesitates, seems to calculate, says, No, I'm afraid I couldn't do that. The policeman has been standing there, looking off into the distance. I ask, either of them really, what I ought to do. I ask whether I oughtn't to see the truck driver's license. No reply. I look toward the policeman. He asks me when I'll be going back to the United States. I say, Friday, or Saturday. He says to the driver, Why don't you give the lady your phone number, and she can call you Friday afternoon. I say, That's fine, but you know, I really ought to have his license number. The policeman says, I'll just write his phone number down for you; asks the driver; writes it down at his dictation. They walk away, as though the matter were at an end. I say, Officer, I think I'll need that rental agreement, if you've finished with it. He says, I returned it to you, I believe. I say, Maybe we left it at the station; and start walking toward the door. I have been standing, as it happens, further from the truck and nearer the station, than either of them. The rental agreement is lying beside the ledger, on the desk. I take it. There is a moment of tension. Then the policeman says, He will have that estimate for you Friday afternoon. The driver smiles. We walk back to the road. As we part, the driver climbs into his cab, smiles again, and says, oddly, You have my word.

Quanta, Amy said, on the train, in that blizzard, in answer to my question. Hello, this is Medea. Wasn't always. Well, he asked for me, you inquired after me, at the conference in the Motel on the Mountain. The motel has since become, what does it matter what it has since become. I don't think they hold conferences there. It is where we began.

Driving onward, I simply do not understand it. What word. Why no exchange of license numbers. There was an undertone, certainly of complicity, but what could possibly have been the underlying calculation? It did not seem, after all, so very cagey to have given me his phone number; better, in some ways, I would have thought, to ask for mine. It was fobbed off, I suppose, in lieu of the driver's license, and of the policeman's actual report. But to what end? I still tend to mistake their apparent lack of intelligence or competence for guilelessness. The policeman never even looked at my car; and if they were planning, for instance, to say that I'd hit and run, why write out the phone number in the officer's own hand? But I do know this: that I ought not to be in the hands of the driver, and the rental agency, and the estimator, for what I'll have to pay. At one point, the driver had said, You know, the damage could be as much as twenty or forty or eighty pounds. I said, surely not as much as that. The policeman said, with a little laugh, You don't know our Irish repairmen. They may have to replace the entire bumper with a new one. And even then, the driver had rejected my offer to pay, whatever it cost, right then and there. I don't know what to do. I would normally call the rental agency, but if the officer has really already called them, that seems redundant; and why was I not called in, why did he not call them in my presence, or look at my car? I have an odd feeling that somehow they do plan to say I've hit and run. But that can't be right. Not when I have that phone number in his handwriting. I know I now need to find an honorable repairman, who will not look at the rental sticker, and proceed to think, as the driver thought, of the agency's insurance. The car, after all, is not due back at the agency for a week. Maybe somebody at the castle will know a repairman. Or maybe Captain Walton, whom the ambassador had mentioned as a special friend and neighbor. I have a small intimation now of danger, and of being, within seconds, entirely at the mercy of unfamiliar people. And I think, Thank goodness it was nothing serious; from one minute to the next everything is changed.

In the pool of the Hospital for Special Surgery, which, perhaps because it specializes in diseases, not of life or death, but of locomotion, must be one of the most cheerful hospitals in the world, we aligned ourselves, at first, naturally, conversationally, according to the gravity of our ailments. The pool room is on the ground floor. Along one wall, its windows look out on the drive and the river, the dazzling grey light and the barges. Nobody swims here, no splashing, no barking or echoing tiles. At the deep end, where the water, which is of course heated, reaches only to the chins of the adults, a young therapist walked slowly back and forth, holding in his extended hands a small wooden bar. Clasping that bar, a small child of about six was being drawn gently, laughing, through the water. Mrs. Martinez, mother of eight, who walked back and forth beside me, looked on with approval; then, in order to free the therapist for other patients, she took over the small bar and the child herself. The three of us were soon joined by Mr. Lanier. It is not quite accurate to say, of Mrs. Martinez, Mr. Lanier, or myself, that we walked. We had been lowered into the pool by means of a crane and stretcher, and now we solemnly proceeded, technically upright and on our feet but with most of our weight borne by the water, from one side to the other of the pool. Anna Mills, who was slightly shorter than we were, walked a little nearer the shallow end, but took part in our general conversation. So, from time to time, did the three young athletes just beyond her. Recovering from knee surgery, they stood, arms outstretched along the pool's edge, bending and straightening their injured legs before them. Buoyantly, gravely, wincing or expressionless, we chatted: about what was wrong with us, how it happened, whether we had been injured, or born this way, or simply, gradually disintegrated; about past surgery, impending surgery, no surgery. But the subject of most profound interest, the one that divided us along lines not of age, or class, or job, or personal affinity, was drugs. The Tylenol set, the group on Empirin with codeine, the poor souls on Bufferin or Darvon, or any non-prescription remedy, were separated from the lucky few on morphine derivatives, on Percodan. The difference, we soon discovered, or rather, the Percodan group discovered it, had less to do with kind of illness or intensity of pain than with the philosophy and disposition of the prescribing doctor. Al Hines, the truck driver, we knew, had been scolded by his doctor for taking too much aspirin, when he had the same problem as Mrs. Martinez, Mr. Lanier, and I. Ten days of traction, Al's doctor had said, and if that didn't do it, surgery. But my own doctor had said that traction—and, in our rooms, all of us were in traction—was of no use whatever, just a device to satisfy insurance companies. So there we were; when Al walked with us, like children discreetly withholding from less enlightened children the truth about the stork or Santa Claus, we would not discuss our medication. And the day old Mrs.

James, completely warped and crabbed by her arthritis into a kind of clawed, bowlegged arc, mentioned that her doctor, bless him, did allow her Percodan, specifically one half a pill four times a day, we, we lucky few who took Percodan (and sometimes, having surreptitiously stored them, three Percodan eight times a day), we said nothing, only continued our stately procession, like swans, or philosophers, generals or Athenians, back and forth across the pool.

But then, stopping everywhere, as I was, to ask directions, it was by no means clear, at many intersections, which was the straight continuation of the road and which was another road entirely. I asked various bicyclists, farmers, passersby. And once, when I pulled far off the road, for the last of several farmers with their herds of lowing cattle, I met, no, not met, encountered, one of the truly gentle and poetic souls, a man who said, You've bent part of your fender against this tall grass; and who bent the metal back in place, along its tidy line, getting mud on his trousers and his hands. A kind man, with the profound sense of natural honor from which, I supposed, the lorry driver's You have my word, in some way, derived. My sense of the ominous and hostile receded. I began to think these were omens, perhaps, after all, auspicious. As the weather let up, I became aware for the first time of serenity, of the fields, the walls of stone, slate sky, the incredibly long eyelashes of the cows. I passed through the countryside, the towns. Just before dark, I found the unpaved road to Cihrbradàn, then the iron gates, and the long drive to the castle. In the circle of gravel, at the front door, I parked my car in such a way that the driver's side, the damaged fender side, was visible to all comers on the road. Later, I thought this even then, later I could say, What kind of fool do you take me for; if concealment was what I had in mind, do you take me for such a fool as to park my car in such a way that the damaged side is there for all the world to see? As I opened the car door and got out, I felt watched. I saw a round middle-aged face peering at me through the shades. Celia, I thought, the hearty cook, looking out eagerly for the first glimpse of the stranger. But, as I crossed the few remaining yards of gravel driveway, she made no move toward the door.

After I had knocked for quite a while, the door was opened by a younger woman. Kathleen, I thought, but when I introduced myself, she did not give her name. She said, There's a note for you from Captain and Mrs. Walton, and led me to a small room, full of guns, boots, hunting jackets, and a large desk. On the wall above the desk, there was an ancient telephone, on a wooden panel, with many wires and switches. An envelope addressed to me lay on the desk. Kathleen handed it to me; and walked back across the little entryway, down a short, narrow corridor, to an immense kitchen, where she introduced me to Celia, who stood beside the kitchen table, watching protectively over a round pink child. You'll be wanting to see your room then, Kathleen said. We climbed a beautiful, old, slowly rounding staircase, to a room which looked out in two directions, on an old grey tower, and on the sea. The waves were placid against the black rocks of the bay; to the absolute verge of those rocks, and the sea itself, the fields extended, in calm, perfect, implausibly familiar, muted green. Three sources of heat in the room, Kathleen pointed out to me briskly: central heating, an electric blanket, the peat fireplace. She also showed me the closet and the bed. Not the bathroom, which I found later, at some distance, down the hall. You'll be wanting tea, she said, as she was going down the staircase. I said, Thank you, yes. And what time would you like your dinner? I looked at my watch. It was five-fifteen. I said, At seven, please. And then, On second thought, with dinner as soon as that, instead of tea, I'd like a drink. I like to go to bed early, I added, and get up early. We walked through the first kitchen, past Celia and the baby, through a second, still larger kitchen, to a pantry, with an enormous wall safe. We always keep it locked, Kathleen said, when the ambassador's away. The door swung open, revealing shelves and quantities of every kind of whiskey, gin, rum, brandy, vodka. As you're his guest, she said, I'll leave the key in while you're here. I chose one of the Irish whiskeys, Bushmills. Have you known the ambassador long? she asked, as she led me through several dark rooms, one of which seemed to be the study, to the drawing room, where the lamps nearest the sofa were on, and there was a peat fire burning in the grate. He had said, Talk to them, they are friendly; so I said, Not long, and told her how I met him, and that he sent his best. Will you be wanting ice? she said. She brought cubes, in a glass, and some water in a small pewter pitcher. I stayed a long time, alone, with my drink, beside the grate in the drawing room. I opened the envelope from Captain and Mrs. Walton. An invitation to dinner, the following evening, at eight. Paddy, the groundskeeper there, will give you directions, it said. Hope you can come. An illegible signature. A legible phone number. One digit, like the number of the castle. I sloshed a bit more water from the pitcher into my glass. A little tired now, from the whiskey, and the day itself, I thought I should call to accept. I found my way to the hunting and phone room, looked at the wooden panel, with its wires and switches. Celia appeared in the doorway. I'd like to phone the Waltons, I said. I can't figure out quite how this works. Kathleen does that, Celia said. A pause. She's upstairs. Feeding the baby. Shall I call her down? I say, It's nothing urgent. Another pause. Celia walks to the phone, turns a crank, flips several switches, then hands the receiver to me. So glad you're here, says the Captain; heard all about you; look forward enormously; just ask Paddy for directions; eight o'clock then. Hangs up. Celia stands in doorway. Whenever you're ready, she says. Your dinner's there.

I look at you for signs of leaving me and find to my despair that one of us has already left. Maybe it's me. But, if it's me, I always do come back, or always have. Please don't go. Writing is always, in part, bending somebody's ear. As reading is. In the matter of the commas. In the matter of the question marks. In the matter of the tenses. In the matter of the scandal at the tennis courts.

But then, don't you see, I despaired. I simply, no, not simply, I rarely do anything simply, despaired. And then I despaired.

In the dining room, my place is set, back to the windows, at one end of the table, which is long. Along the wall at the opposite end of the table is a massive sideboard, on which there is a silver bowl of fruit. On the table, to the left of my plate, is a small electric bell. From the kitchen, Kathleen brings in oxtail soup, which is very hot. Before I have finished, she brings in a serving tray with

five lamb chops, also mashed potatoes, string beans, squash, all
home grown. Five lamb chops seems a lot for a single guest. I eat
two, wonder ever so briefly who will eat the others. Kathleen comes
in with a crème caramel large enough to serve, I guess, twenty
people. When I ask for seconds, having for the first time used the
electric bell, Kathleen returns with the immense dish, on which
half a single portion now remains. I am really tired, and perhaps
slightly crocked. As I pass the kitchen, on my way to the stairs,
Celia says, What time will you be wanting breakfast? I say, Don't
trouble with breakfast; I like to go to sleep very early, and get up
very early. Kathleen says, We come in at nine-thirty, but you just
sleep in late. That subject seems closed somehow. But before I say
goodnight, I ask, Is there anything I need to know about the peat
fire in my room: I mean, do I just use a match? Kathleen says yes.
When I reach my room, there are no matches. I return to the
drawing room, find matches beside the grate, go back upstairs to my
room, and try match after match against the peat, to no effect. I go
downstairs to the kitchen, say, Somehow the matches don't quite
seem to work. Oh well, Kathleen says, of course you need the firestarter. She walks into a room, which, when she turns the light on,
turns out to be the study, hands me a packet of brown squares,
in color and texture rather like what was served to us in college
as scrapple. I take the packet to my room, put one of the squares
against the peat and light it. The fire takes, immediately. Soon the
room is hot. I open the window slightly, upon the luminous sea-
scape and the tower; I do not shut the drapes against the sky. Putting blankets, pillow, sheets on the carpeted floor, beside the grate,
I fall asleep almost at once, coughing slightly, from the smoldering
peat perhaps, or the air coming through the windows. I think of the
coughing man on the plane, and then, with a smile, of the serious-
ness with which our night editor, at the paper, regards what his
secretary refers to as his little colds. When I wake up, well before
dawn, I am warm. The sky is still blue-black; and yet sea, rocks,
green verge, and tower are irradiated, clear. I have begun to love
the beauty, and the quiet. To begin with, after all, I almost went
instead to Graham Island. Not to have to wait for you any more,
your call, the sound, as characteristic as your footsteps, of your

engine in the driveway, what that would mean. Not to think of you all the time any more. And suddenly I welcomed grey weather, clouds and rain.

What's new? the biography of the opera star says she used to ask in every phone call, and What else? I'm not sure the biographer understood another thing about the opera star, but I do believe that What's new. What else. They may be the first questions of the story, of the morning, of consciousness. What's new. What else. What next. What's happened here, says the inspector, or the family man looking at the rubble of his house. What's it to you, says the street tough or the bystander. What's it *worth* to you, says the paid informer or the extortionist. What is it now, says the executive or the husband, disturbed by the fifteenth knock at the door, or phone call, or sigh in the small hours of the night. What does it mean, says the cryptographer. What does it all mean, says the student or the philosopher on his barstool. What do I care. What's the use. What's the matter. Where's the action. What kind of fun is that. Let me say that everyone's story in the end is the old whore's, or the Ancient Mariner's: I was not always as you see me now. And the sentient man, the sentient person says in his heart, from time to time, What have I done.

Was it in the contemplation of my ancestors that I should share a guest room, one long weekend, with Mausi Esterhazi? Was it in the contemplation of Mausi's ancestors. Was it in the contemplation of my ancestors that the sushi chef should say to me, with concern, at summer's end, You are lose weight? Or that one curator should say to another, in my presence, of a third, He is married, which is very important in Chicago?

You spend too much time alone, says a murmur from the anticlaque; you are like some wet, tousled, obsessed rat or mouse, in a concrete bunker, all the time alone. But also, you spend too much time with friends. Here we have the water colors, here we have the bas reliefs. And these are the oils. This is the sculpture garden. We also have mobiles, in color, that can both make sounds and move. And here, he said, we have the rubble that resulted when the breakthrough came. You remember everything, he said, you remember everything, out of context, and then you brood. Look, you can't write on a trapeze, and this is not a metronome. Yes, it is. I live with an hysteric and a metronome. I live with a person in despair. I live on a trapeze in a jungle where there is a harpsichord. I'm a pretty persuasive advocate when the cause is just.

When I have dressed and gone downstairs, I find a small pitcher of milk in the refrigerator; on a shelf, nearby, an open jar of instant coffee, two-thirds empty, with a spoon still in it, clearly Celia's. Everything else is clean, tidy, spankingly empty. In a small, damp pantry, not the one with the wall safe, I find a trash can, full of coffee grounds and egg shells. For the compost heap, I think. No eggs. On the counter, some stale bread. Though the kitchen is very well equipped, with pots, pans, stoves, refrigerators, small devices, even, come to think of it, elaborate hi-fi radio (Celia, I now recall, had, from the moment I met her, been playing loud, incongruous rock), I cannot, for some reason, find the toaster. I know there must be one. I try the oven. After several minutes of looking in vain for the pilot light, with matches, I give up. Fearing an explosion, I turn the oven off, and consider giving a toaster as a house present. I make coffee, with hot water from the tap and cold milk from the pitcher. I decide to try to use the telephone. Having turned the crank, and figured out the switches, I reach an operator, to whom I explain that, once my call has gone through to New York, he must under no circumstances interrupt the call, because to do so would be to disrupt, perhaps permanently, but at the very least for half an hour, my answering machine. Oh, he says, I would never interrupt; I only connect you with the international operator. Then, bypassing the international operator, he puts the call straight through, and abruptly cuts it off. When I try again, having waited the required half hour, I reach the international operator. In response to my explanation, she says, becoming very obdurate on this point, I would never cut into a line, certainly, never. As soon as the call goes through, she breaks in, to say, Go ahead please, your party is on the line. When another half hour has elapsed, I reach her again. I start to say, But this time, operator, please. And she says, with that edge of injury and contempt I am beginning to become accustomed to in all their voices: It was only a recording. The call goes through. No message there.

She was Goldilocks, really, with this exception: when the third bear left, he had taken with him his porridge, and his chair. And the bed? Well, the bed was there, and the prince came and he kissed her. Hey, wait. Look here, this is Medea. This is Eloise at the Plaza. This is Agatha Runcible. Here I am, for the first time, and yet again, alone at last on Orcas Island. You were, you know, you are the nearest thing to a real story to happen in my life, and you are gone.

I go into the study, light a peat fire, watch the dawn through the soft rain. From the bookshelves, I take down Samuel Pepys, abridged; I have somehow never read him. I put paper in the typewriter, and begin a friendly note to the ambassador. Shortly after ten, the front door opens. I hear voices in the kitchen. I find Celia, Kathleen, that overfed, moon-faced baby, all three eating fried eggs and ham. I mention that I have had coffee with milk. Was there enough for you? Celia says, perhaps with irony, certainly not in the slightest friendly. Or what would you like for breakfast now. I say I'd like a five-minute egg. And, when Kathleen brings it to me, at my place in the dining room, the egg really is five minutes. Celia had not mentioned toast, nor had I, so I'm startled when, as I eat in silence, toast pops up out of a toaster, which I had simply not noticed on the sideboard. I get up, take the toast and a banana. When I have finished eating, I return to the study. As I begin to type, Kathleen appears, says, Will you be wanting me for your phone calls? I say, Thank you, I think I can manage. About an hour later, a stocky man, in a woolen cap and jacket, comes in, says, How do you do, I'm Paddy. Is there anything I can do for you this morning? He seems marginally more friendly than the others. At the same time, something covertly appraisive in his manner, an almost lascivious shrewdness, makes me think, Is it just that they think I'm the ambassador's mistress, and that there is something not quite proper in the arrangement; is it my clothes, the faded corduroy slacks, the tennis shoes, my down jacket; or, perhaps outdoors, the damaged fender? But I say, Well, yes, Paddy, could you tell me the best place to go for a walk. How long a walk were you thinking of? he says. I say, About an hour, and add that I don't have much sense of direction. In some detail, then, he describes a walk. I ask where I would go if I wanted a two-hour walk. In reply, he describes what I realize is the exact same walk. While it's true I've said that I can get lost virtually anywhere, on account of that sense of direction, it seems odd to me, not sinister but odd, that the one-hour walk and the two-hour walk should be the same. As I pass the kitchen, on my way to the front door, Celia asks what I would like for lunch. Remembering the ambassador's words, I ask whether I might have a picnic. Celia, brightening, says, Now? I look at my watch. It is quarter past eleven. I say, No thank you, when I come back from this walk, I'll just take another walk and have my picnic then. I set out down the driveway, toward a path along the sea verge and the rocks. When the path turns inland, uphill, the wind subsides, the rain slows to a fine mist, and I see, coming toward me, a small man of middle years, with one of the sad, poetic faces— wisdom there, humor and beauty. From some distance off, he says, Good morning, in such a friendly voice. I reply, Good morning. And, not wanting to lose contact, I go on, Nice day. A bit showery, he says, as he steps aside to let me pass. We continue on our separate ways.

In the matter of solipsism and prayer. It makes no sense, of course, to pray if you alone exist, and there is no world outside your consciousness, unless you think of prayer as just a kind of song. A lonely song. But if you pray to something, and for something, it is also, I think, a solipsistic thing to pray to affect an outcome which, though still unknown, is already quite set. If you are a determinist, of course, then everything is and forever has been set, and all your prayers are songs. Not lonely songs, perhaps, but songs. The sort of prayer I mean, though, is the more ordinary kind: the devout expression of a wish, with a real intent to influence an outcome of some sort. And such a prayer, to be reasonable in a world where there are others, must address consequences that are truly and altogether in the future. It would be solipsistic, for example, to pray that the outcome of a test already taken will be this or that, or to affect the set result of any act already past. Such a prayer, though it has the appearance of reasonable anticipation, is already somewhat retroactive, a prayer for a miraculous revision of the past. While there's nothing wrong with the miraculous, it always requires an abrogation of the law in one's own special case: when it is also retroactive, it has an additional, though perhaps unconscious, solipsism at its heart. The tense, the perfected future of it, is the clue. You can pray that things will be other than as they were, other than they are. The forbidden, the solipsistic tense is this: that things *will have been* other than they were. Prayer must be timely and it must be prompt. Not even in a world of miracles, and only if the world is yours alone, can you pray the past away.

And the virtuoso, and the pachysandra, and love long ago, and the awful night of Eva dancing? "The only invitation to leave a road," Judge Holmes once said, in a famous court decision, "is at its end." The case involved what is called in law an attractive nuisance, something hazardous, an uncovered blade or well, an unattended piece of machinery, which might tempt a child to stray and hurt himself. The children in the Holmes case were more than hurt, they fell into a lake of chemicals and were dissolved. But the more one looks at the great judge's words, the more clearly they are an instance of the hollow, perfectly specious aphorism. The one place at which roads normally extend no invitation whatsoever is at their ends. Every road's invitation seems to lie either on it, as a means to reach a destination, or alongside, where its own destinations, diners, shops, and houses, are. At the end of a road, there is usually, at best, an intersection with another road. More commonly, there is nothing. Or a quarry, or a reservoir.

The Olive Pell Bible, one of the best-selling Bibles of its time though not perhaps in history, was an expurgated Bible. Mrs. Pell had begun by crossing out and removing from the Bibles of her friends any passage with a carnal implication, including, to name just one example, the begats. The result, as it turned out, was a very short, dense text. Her friends soon urged Mrs. Pell to give the public the benefit of all the talent and industry required for such a condensation, and so the Olive Pell Bible went into the first of its many printings. It is very hard to obtain a copy now.

An hour later, I am back, from my walk, in my own room at the castle. On the rug, in the hallway, outside a room two doors from mine, I have noticed a pail, an empty bottle of Evian water, and a towel. In discussing the routine of the castle, the ambassador said, I now remember, Kathleen will give you bottled water. There was no bottled water in my room, and the water, not just from the taps, but also in the glass beside my plate at table, I have also noticed, is distinctly brown. I don't mind brown water, having used it on visits to friends in South Carolina and Georgia; I had even rather liked the sulphur smell. Nonetheless, there is now something disturbing, something in the nature, can it be? of a statement, or declaration, about that empty Evian bottle. I hear Celia's voice and Kathleen's nearby, and I think, It is nothing, jet lag maybe or a hangover. They are cleaning out a room. What could be more normal than a pail, an empty bottle, and a towel. I look around my room, rearrange a few things in the closet, put on a dry pair of shoes and socks. In the basket which holds the peat beside the fireplace, I now notice several spent, old, yellowed cigarette stubs. Though they are clearly remnants of some earlier visit, I wonder whether it will somehow be thought that they are mine. Not wanting to be thought that sort of guest, and also from an innate sense that they just don't belong there, I start to rummage in the peat and pick them out. When I have gathered the first handful of these crumpled objects, along with their bits of loose tobacco, I become aware of what I begin now to consider a distinct air of growing conspiracy. I hope that the ambassador will remember, even on the basis of our few and short encounters, that I do not smoke. Perhaps this is the moment when the fantasy, or paranoia, or whatever it is, sets in in earnest, only in reverse, as a form of faith: faith that the ambassador, when he sees or hears about these filthy cigarette ends, will recall that I am not a smoker, and therefore cannot be to blame for them. So, getting the hang of this castle war, if war it is, of stubbornnesses; not knowing, anyway, where else to put them; and having more difficulty than I thought extricating all the remaining stubs and stray remnants of tobacco, I rebury them now among the peat.

When I go downstairs, the kitchen is empty. On the table, I find the picnic lunch box—rather like the pails, with buckles, which we used to take our lunch to school in. I set out again on my walk.

Where the path veers uphill from the sea, I continue along the sea's edge. Though I am damp and chilled, I find a large flat rock, sheltered from the wind by other rocks. From the cup of the thermos I drink soup, the same oxtail soup they served last night at dinner, but so hot that it burns as it goes down. Good, I imagine, for what remains of my slight cough. The sandwiches are white bread with ham, the same ham they were frying with their eggs at breakfast. There is also a tomato sandwich, an orange, a hardboiled egg. I eat and drink all this hunkered among the rocks. In a corner of the kitchen, when I first met Celia, there had been a tall, stooped man, whom I took to be Pat. He did not speak, and we were not introduced. Now, on my return, this silent man is working, with a power saw, under Paddy's supervision, just inside the gravel circle. He pauses, smiles at me, waves, and resumes his work. I mention to Paddy that the Waltons have invited me to dinner, and that the Captain said to ask Paddy for directions to their house. Paddy thinks, says, I can't, starts to give directions, breaks off, says, I can't, you see, I've lived here all my life. This makes a kind of sense. Many people find it hard to give directions, when they are too familiar with the way. At the same time, it seems odd, since both the ambassador and the Waltons have designated Paddy as a guide. I know, he says, why don't you ask Kathleen. Her boy is at school not far from there. You can follow her when she goes to pick him up. I ask when that will be. Late this afternoon, he says; but then adds, very slowly and firmly, You must go and ask her now. I go upstairs, where the pail, the dirty white towel and the empty Evian bottle are still on the hallway rug, and I walk into the room where Kathleen and Celia are. They don't look up. When I ask, Kathleen says she picks up the child half past two, quarter to three. Paddy's idea, perhaps, of late afternoon. As I lie down, in my room, to rest and perhaps read a bit, I begin to review whether these can really be what I must regard as a virtual campaign of intransigences. The business of the firestarter and the matches, the immense then suddenly diminished dessert, even the question whether I've known the ambassador long, now range beside the lack of bottled water, the unlighted lamps, the resistance, when I arrived, in the matter of the phone. I think, It's absurd, it is just that I've been too long alone. My sense that there is something wrong in the course of these events begins, after all, with the small matter of the car; and, in the matter of the car, it is I who am at fault. I look toward the grate. No matches. No firestarter. Crumpled cigarette ends. I hear a car start, go to the window, see behind the wheel a sweatered bosom, assume it is Kathleen. As I walk downstairs, and see that the car is already at the far end of the driveway, I think, I am going to leave this country and this house.

When the clouds shift, for one moment, or for several moments, and there is a possibility for action with absolutely no ingredient of reluctance—any action, shopping, playing tennis, getting out of bed—when there is a sense of the capacity to act, without any equal and dialectical incapacity to act, or desire not to, when the urge to move is, for a moment, some moments, freed of the urge to move another way, or not to move at all, or the drag of a rock, a doubt, a paralysis; then it is as though clouds did part, briefly, in a place where the climate is always and always inimical. There are, of course, sadnesses that appear to consist of a stillness heaped upon a stillness, layers of apathy, over a base that is despair and lack of hope. Despair *and* lack of hope, because lack of hope is by no means incompatible with the cloudless and the free state. Witness Ben and the swami, and the people at the ashram, without hope but in a state of bliss. But if the state, the condition, the zone, the tenor of spirit, where no light shines lacks any ingredient either of calm or of expectation, there are also depressions of which the appearance is jaunty, counterdepressive. That is, the degree to which the creature is able to act, or to permit itself to be seen, reflects such a surface play of the energy, which, in its perfect conflict, has brought to the paralysis an almost convulsive force, that the energy appears active, liberated, even cheerful. Analysis has no access to this condition. It poses very radically, however, the question of what it is to be sincere.

You can see it from here; but just try to get to it.

What you want, don't you see, what you want is, under the conscious pressures, a surprise within the rules.

We all find we cannot take on any more patients. We are all waiting for calls from superiors, pick up the phones each time hoping it is one of them, then find it is only another patient. The superiors of course think of us as patients and dread our calls.

Is it always the same story, then? Somebody loves and somebody doesn't, or loves less, or loves someone else. Or someone is a
good soul and someone a villain. And there are just these episodes,
anecdotes, places, pauses, hailings of cabs, overcomings of obstacles,
or instances of being overcome by them, illnesses, accidents, re-
coveries, wars, desires, welcomings, rebuffs, baskings (rare, not so
long), pinings (more frequent, perhaps, and longer), actions, failures to act, hesitations, proliferations, endings of the line, until
there is death. Well, no. I have a wonderful, fond memory, about
love and trust and *books*. I mean, a dog wrote back to me. I mean,
the book ended with an invitation to write letters to the dog, and
contained, on its inside back cover, a packet of three sheets of paper
and three envelopes. I wrote to the dog three times, and three
times he wrote back. I also wrote again, and was a little disappointed
when the days passed and no answer came. But it was explained to
me, or I somehow understood it, or perhaps expected that *someday*,
when he had time and got around to it, I would hear from him
again. And of course by the time I realized I had not heard and
would probably not hear again, I understood completely and also
I had grown up. The contrast, after all, with Tom McDermott, the
swimming instructor, who used to call himself Tom McDermo-
witz, which I, never having heard of Jews or knowing that we were
Jews, did not understand; his writing me a note that enclosed an
intermediate swimmers card, which I already had in any event, and
why, come to think of it, did he write to me at all, or why not send
what he promised, or, looked at another way, why did he not
realize that my parents, if they had been that sort of parents, might
have made trouble for him at that Florida hotel. My father always
said that it is a reasonable expectation of life that no one will go out
of his way, against his own interest, to break his word or to hurt
another person. And this turns out, not just in obvious cases, for
example haters, pathological people and institutions, sadists, but in
everyday life itself to be plain untrue. I wonder why. A reasonable
expectation of life, I have found, is hardly ever quite borne out.

As I walk downstairs, and I see that the car is already at the
far end of the driveway, I think, I am going to leave this country
and this house. Maybe things will be better, though, at dinner.

Maybe the Waltons will change the apparent course and character of these events. I intend, however, to ask them about ferries out of Dublin (as opposed, that is, to my return flight out of Shannon); I have begun to think steadily now, in other words, in terms of escape. I consider, too, whether to use a wet towel, that towel for instance lying upstairs on the rug, to remove the rental sticker from the rear window of the car. Whether this has to do with what I might be charged at a repair shop, or simply with becoming inconspicuous, in case I should be followed, is not yet clear. I return to my room, pack the smaller of my bags, and take it downstairs, hoping to put it quietly into the car. In the front hallway, however, I encounter Kathleen. I was just coming to look for you, she says, I'm leaving now. So I put my suitcase on a hallway chair. As soon as I get in my car, and turn the key in the ignition, Kathleen takes off, racing down the castle driveway. When we turn into the public road, she hits speeds over sixty miles an hour. The road has many curves and intersections. I try slowing down, to lag behind. She speeds nearly out of sight. So I give up, and race along, to follow closely, on flat open stretches, at crossroads, on narrow curves. Perhaps, I think, it is only high spirits, perhaps she always drives this way. Suddenly, without any signal, she veers left and screeches to a halt at what appears to be an unattended gas pump. Needed fuel, she says. I wait, while she tugs at the hose and fills the tank. She roars off, accelerates further, then, abruptly, not even pulling over this time, stops. I stop. She gets out of her car. It's up there, she says, gesturing vaguely toward a small crossroad, leading off the highway. It has no distinguishing features, so far as I can tell, except perhaps for a No Dumping sign, which faces the opposite way from the way I shall be coming from. How will I ever find this in the dark? I ask. I wondered that, she says. A silence. She says, We passed a little bridge back there. Where? I ask. Back there a bit, she says. It's the first crossroad right after that little bridge. She gets in her car, and speeds along her way.

I return slowly along the road, and find the almost imperceptible overpass which she calls a bridge. I notice, too, that it is where the painted road divider stops. I watch the mileage, from that bridge, until I reach what becomes for me a landmark of a sort, a rundown service station, with signs for Exxon and Toyota. I wonder briefly whether this might be the place to have my car repaired. From bridge to service station: 1.9 miles. Then, eight more miles to the Cihrbradàn turnoff. Even by daylight I scarcely find it. At the castle, I wonder whether to call the Waltons and ask them to come and get me, think they must be old and frail and that is why they have not offered. In my room, I start to pack in my second, larger bag, all the things but those that would most badly wrinkle. I become aware that all the lights are off. I turn on a few lamps, wonder whether to have a drink, decide not to. There is no note, from Kathleen or Celia, about locking up. The house seems particularly silent. The pail, with the towel and the empty bottle, is still in the hallway, two doors from my room. Everyone has apparently left for the night, and I become aware that I'm alone. I go downstairs, take my suitcase from the hallway chair, and go outside to put it in my car. As I lean over the back seat, I look more closely at the rental sticker, which is affixed to the inside of the rear window. It had already, dimly, crossed my mind to use that hallway towel, soaked, but now I pull tentatively at the transparent edge of the sticker, and find the whole thing peels right off. I fold it, roll it up and put it in the pocket of my slacks. I become aware that this move at last is irreversible. The sticker now adheres to itself. I think how I might explain it: worry about overcharge in a repair shop, based on a mistake about insurance. I rehearse a little speech; it sounds all right. Maybe, at this point, it is still true. On the way back to my room, I pass through the study, pick up my unfinished note to the ambassador, close the typewriter, go upstairs to take a little nap. Through the window that looks out on the tower, I notice a man in a yellow raincoat, walking in the general direction of the gatehouse. Paddy, I know, lives in the gatehouse, and it crosses my mind that he may have reported the peeling and removal of the object now rolled up and stuck together in my pocket, and that the man in the yellow raincoat may be a local policeman, coming to check. I can hardly throw the thing away, with them both out there; and it can hardly be illegal to have a car rental sticker temporarily upon one's person. I decide, after all, to have a drink. I go downstairs, and find the Bushmills still on the side-

board in the drawing room. There is no ice, of course, but there is
also no water in the pewter pitcher, no fire in the grate, and no firestarter in the basket. My cough returns. I become aware that I have
not been feeling well. As I sit on the fender, near the slightly smoldering peat, which I have managed to ignite with matches, I wonder
whether it would after all be best to pack my remaining things, put
them in the car, and set out for the airport that night, directly from
the Waltons. I think not. Maybe, if they are nice, for instance, or
can give me advice about repairmen, I won't leave at all. At least,
I think again, I have at last done something. I have come this far;
maybe everything will still be well. If not, it would be best to set out
very early in the morning, after a few hours' sleep. But I am still
uneasy. So I go to the phone room, and begin to call the airlines. I
have already confirmed my flight from Shannon, Friday, the return
flight on my ticket. I now book another flight, out of Dublin, giving
a different first initial with my name. I call British Airways, Dublin;
and without giving any name at all (but, of course, all calls on this
phone go via the local operator; and the ambassador had said to me,
half joking, Don't try to discuss any private matters on that phone,
they're listening in), I ask what flights there are on Thursday.
Which, I suddenly realize, is tomorrow. There are four flights, two
British Airways, two Aer Lingus. I imagine flying the Irish national
airline may make one more clearly subject to the laws of Ireland,
and its jurisdiction. I prefer to avoid the Irish flights. I ask whether
the British Airways morning flight is open, am told it is. I make no
reservation on it, thinking I now have two Friday reservations, one
from Shannon, one from Dublin. If they look for me, they will be
looking for me Friday. Meanwhile, I intend to make that open
Thursday morning flight.

I go back upstairs to dress. I set off for the Waltons' early, leaving time to drive very slowly, and even to get lost. There is a strong
wind, and driving sleet. I can hardly see, with those thirteen-second
wipers. I wonder again whether the Waltons are too frail, or perhaps too short of staff, to send someone to get me. I find the Exxon-
Toyota station; exactly 1.9 miles later, the bridge, the end of the
painted white divider, and the turnoff. Almost immediately, on

this little side road, there is a fork. I had thought, and the expression is entirely uncharacteristic of me, that bitch, when Kathleen had sped off and refused to slow down, even when I slowed and she nearly lost me, but I'd also thought, no, maybe with her it's just high spirits, and she doesn't see the problem when someone is trying just to follow and to learn the way. But now, the fork, when she had only said, It's up there, waving vaguely. I thought, well, it wasn't just high spirits. I chose to bear left. After a long time, with a sense of the sea very close beside me, in that darkness, I approached a high wall, almost a fortification, with, behind it, a small house and one dim light. I wondered why the Waltons, expecting a guest, would not have lighted their place more brightly, decide they would have, pass along the fortification, reach another fork. There are, in addition to the two paved branches, two dirt roads, or driveways, one marked Cul de Sac, the other, perhaps more improbably, Danger Taureaux. I turn around. The sea is now on my left, on the passenger's side. I enter the drive that leads into the fortification, park, walk to the house with the single lighted window, knock at the door. No answer. From inside, I can hear, muted, a television set. I am now quite loudly knocking. Finally, I try the door. It opens directly into a kitchen, where a man and a small boy are watching television. I apologize, ask for directions to the Waltons'. And the man tells me, in that crazy, unclear Irish way, just to follow the road I have been on and, at the nearest fork, bear the equivalent of straight. I turn in the driveway, which is narrow. The man stands in the doorway, making the sounds, and even the physical gestures, which men of all classes, the world over, seem to make to a woman, who is simply putting her car into reverse to turn or park it, when they say, as if this were a piece of arcane wisdom, never before heard by woman, Cut it, cut it hard. I say thank you. Then, not unlike Kathleen, yes unlike her, but because the car has now entirely lost its second gear, I roar off. A mile or two past the fork, I find a drive which I somehow take to be the Waltons'. This house has two lights, both dim. Since they are widely separated, it is not clear which marks the entrance of the house. I choose one. Again, I am in a kitchen. A woman, in her early forties, with straight blond hair hanging to her shoulders, comes in from a hall-

way, says, I'm Nicole Walton. Clem's not ready. You must be
Kate. I look at my watch, and realize I've left myself too much
time. I am ten minutes early. I have recognized Nicole's accent at
once. It is Berlin. She is wearing a dark woolen skirt and sweater.
She leads me to a very comfortable drawing room, with shabby
pretty furniture and oriental carpets, seats me beside the fireplace.
She offers me an Irish whiskey, which I accept. She says, I'll bring
some ice. I say, Thank you, no ice. She asks me where I am from.
Before I can reply, she says, The ambassador has told us all about
you. Then, she asks me why I've come to Cihrbradàn. I say, I was
looking for somewhere beautiful and quiet, on the sea. To my surprise, I add, Where I can rest. Captain Walton walks in, very brisk,
stocky and hearty, looking at his watch. I was just cutting my toenails, he says, it's a very auspicious hour for cutting toenails. I take
it this is his form of witticism, small talk, earthiness. We shake
hands. Nicole says, Kate and I were just talking about all the places
she must visit during the short time she is in Ireland. We had, of
course, been talking of nothing of the sort. I say, No, actually, it's
Cihrbradàn I've come to, just for the quiet, and to rest. But somehow they do not seem to hear this. They immediately take up their
own conversation about places I must visit. They agree that Clem
will take me tomorrow, first thing in the morning, to a place he has
loved since his boyhood, called, for reasons they now elaborate,
Mummy's beach. I ask Nicole where she is from. She says Chicago,
with what is so clearly a German o that I'm taken aback. I just say,
Really. She says, Before that Minneapolis. I have now firmly decided that by tomorrow I shall be gone from Ireland. As I wonder
exactly what I am going to do about this, the phone rings. Nicole
goes into another room to answer it, comes back, says to Clem, that
was Judy, from London; and to me, she was going to come this
weekend. Judy loves Ireland as much as you and Clem and I do,
but with this latest business of the IRA, the silly girl's afraid to
come. Clem says, It's just the newspapers; Kate knows all about
the newspapers. I say, with some interest, But I haven't read a
newspaper in days. We hear footsteps in the hall. Clem calls out,
Hello, William, Iris. And another couple come in, Americans.
When Clem has introduced us, and brought their drinks, with ice,
he also brings me another, very large, whiskey. This one, too, with

ice. Nicole says to the couple, We were just discussing where Kate should go, on her Irish tour. She's going with Clem tomorrow, to Mummy's beach.

And this matter of the commas. And this matter of the paragraphs. The true comma. The pause comma. The afterthought comma. The hesitation comma. The rhythm comma. The blues. And in this matter of the tenses and the question marks. In this matter of the scandal at the tennis courts. Did he know so little, then, of love that he did not know that the experience he has put me through, all those times, in all those years, is the one I've adumbrated, for a few hours, from time to time, just now?

Nicole says, to the American couple, We were just discussing where Kate should go, on her Irish tour; she's going with Clem tomorrow, to Mummy's beach. I say, No, it turns out that I must go to London, for just one day. Coming back the same night, or maybe the following morning, and I'm afraid tomorrow will have to be the day. I am now trying to establish with these people my absolute intention not just to leave, but to return, within hours, to Ireland; so I stress it. I want there to be no question, or at least less question, of my attempting to flee the jurisdiction, if I'm caught, the word caught, and my problem, are becoming definite to me, along the way. Clem and Nicole give a little pantomime of despairing fondness, and then become distinctly bullying. I must postpone my trip to London until the last day of my stay in Ireland; under no circumstances can I go as soon as tomorrow. But by this time it has turned out that William, before retiring from his American professorship of physiology, had worked as a consultant to the United Nations. William now mentions that a UN official, a man much in the news, has arrived that day in Paris. As it happens, I know that official very well. I say, with surprising conviction, that the reason I must go tomorrow is that I have to interview him. Since the man in question has considerable chic and power, Clem somehow overlooks the question of why I must go to London to interview an official who has just arrived in Paris. I am not too much worried by this apparent inconsequence. We have all had at least three drinks by now, and as we walk to the dining room, Clem takes my arm.

As soon as you get back, then, he says, the day after tomorrow, you and I will go to Mummy's beach. The ambassador has told us everything about you. Nicole and I, you know, own some property in common. Mummy's beach, actually. And when he wrote to us, the ambassador said, Kate will know just the sort of people to buy the property. People who would fit in, he says, squeezing my arm. You know, *des gens convenables.* I think, Good heavens, can I have heard him right? I say, Oh yes, what an interesting idea.

We sit down at the dinner table, Nicole, William, Iris, Clem, and I. William is the first to get distinctly voluble and drunk. A meal, it is clear, has been laid on at considerable expense: smoked salmon, Russian vodka, very good wine, mutton, a wide variety of vegetables. There may be a cook, but it seems there is no other staff. We serve ourselves from the sideboard. The conversation turns somehow to Irish politics, nothing to do with what might come to mind, in the rest of the world, in connection with Irish politics, but rather this: the effect the European Economic Community has had on the natural laziness of the Irish working man. Every time I take a sip of wine, Nicole looks meaningfully at Clem, and at my wine glass, and he refills it. They seem to have no worry whether I can safely drive at all, let alone find my way home, home, in the dark, having drunk as much as this. Membership in the European Economic Community, they have all agreed, has totally undermined what vestige there was of a will to work among the Irish poor. But Iris, now, is clearly lit, on the Stolichnaya; she embarks upon a complicated story about a bearded young man, who had come, with two assistants, to do some work at her place, the cottage in which she and William have lived since William retired. The bearded young man was always late; repairs were much delayed. One day, when Iris asked him why, he said that he and his crew also had three other jobs. And the worst of it, she adds, is that on Thursdays he could never come; because that was the day he had to go and collect his check. He was on the dole. A silence. I call that point, set, *and* match, she says. A reminiscence from William about life as a physiologist in Uganda. From Nicole, some thoughts about the vicissitudes of country life. Strangely brutal, her anecdotes are, considering that her declared theme is the peacefulness of this place, the country, how she could never return to city life back home in Chicago.

Meanwhile, she tells about the day when she looked away for one minute, and the gander pecked all his progeny to death. About the cow, which she had noticed was becoming weak, too weak perhaps to survive another winter. How she, Nicole, had put a halter on the cow, and walked it to the butcher. About the ill luck which caused the cow to drop dead right on the butcher's doorstep. And about the technicality, the pedantry, the obtuseness that led the butcher to maintain that he could not sell meat from a cow that had arrived already dead. Nicole had twisted its tail. She swore that the animal flinched. But the butcher denied he had seen it move, and refused to slaughter it. Nicole giggles, and sighs again over the expense of such a cow. She tells of the time the sheep were poisoned; of the time her son, grown now but still a baby then, was bitten by a dog no one could find. She speaks of the pain of rabies shots. From time to time, with ever greater insistence, there recurs as well, between Clem and Nicole, a kind of multi-national name-dropping duet, and then a return to the subject of property in this idyllic part of Ireland. And Mummy's beach. Iris and William, very tipsy but apparently prepared, exclaim and agree, whenever either of our hosts looks in their direction. But then, Nicole says, When I was a child, and Papa, of course, was a conductor. William, from the depths of his cups, says, helpfully, Orchestral? And Nicole, annoyed, perhaps, at the interruption, says, U-Boat. There is a pause. She says, more improbably still, In those days, everyone's Papa was. Back home in Chicago? I wonder, or Minneapolis?

After dinner, the men and the women separate briefly, to different bedrooms, the men downstairs, the women upstairs, the two places, apparently, where the bathrooms are. It is bitter cold in the upstairs bedroom, and there is something in its shabbiness, and perhaps in the fact that the windows are lined against drafts by sopping towels, which suggests a need, after all, of money in this house. And as Nicole, having shown us to the bathroom, goes downstairs, Iris suddenly turns to me and says, very softly and with real kindness, If for some reason, when you come back from London, you'd feel more comfortable staying with us, I mean with William and me, well, it's only a small cottage, compared to the castle, or to this house, but we have an extra bedroom. I thank her.

For some reason, we have been talking almost in a whisper. Nicole returns. We fall silent, and go downstairs In the hall, outside the drawing room, conversation is desultory. Though Iris and William have also been saying goodbye, and putting on their coats, I am in fact the first to leave. They watch from the doorway, as I turn the car around in yet another narrow driveway. There is heavy rain, which turns to snow. By some miracle, I find my way back to the intersection with the main road. As I turn into it, the snow stops, the night is clear. I am worried that I will not find the Cihrbradàn turnoff, so I watch the road for any sign. There are no other cars at all. After several miles, however, there is just one car, coming toward me. We are on the straightaway, and the distance between us is at first considerable; but soon we are close, and no matter how far I pull over to the right, halfway up finally on the embankment, we seem nearer to collision. When we brake, both incredulous, to a halt, virtually headlight to headlight, I see that the man at the wheel of the other car is a priest. Until now, I had been proceeding, in the face of this inexplicable difficulty, almost entirely by instinct. As, of course, had he. And it is only when we brake to our unlikely halt, on the outer edge of a road, just before midnight, that it occurs to me in what way I have been wrong. I make gestures of apology, the priest nods, we back up, and I move to the correct side of the road. I arrive, without further incident, at the castle and my room.

I finish packing, take my things downstairs. As I pass the kitchen, there occurs to me the question of the tips. That is, though I have spent the entire evening trying to establish my intention to return from London before the car's lease has even expired, there is now more than a strong possibility that, if I get safely out of Ireland, I shall not be coming back. Leaving tips, of course, implies that the departure is, in some sense, final. If you really intended to come back within a day, they would say, if they caught me, on the road or at the airport, then you would not have left these tips. But I cannot somehow, whatever our relations may have been, bring myself to go away without leaving something for the staff. So I use the ambassador's typewriter again, to type out envelopes to Kathleen, Paddy, and Celia. And in Celia's envelope I enclose a note, which says: "I have gone overnight," here for some reason

I write, "To Limerick," and I add, "Back Friday, or will call." In my room, I again leave the curtains open, in order to wake up at first light. It is now after midnight. I don't want to take a pill, lest I oversleep. And I cannot sleep. I read a little Samuel Pepys, rather like it. Then I rest. Wanting to leave time to get lost on the way to Dublin, yet not wanting to leave at a suspicious hour, I get up at three A.M., go downstairs, reconsider my note to Celia, cross out "Limerick," write in "London," cross out "London," write in "Away." I drink some milk, feel rather sick from the thickness and richness of it; make some coffee, drink that with warm milk, feel marginally better. I get the Irish whiskey from the drawing room, put it in the pantry safe, lock the safe, think it might be insulting to put the key on the kitchen table beside the envelopes, leave the key on the counter beside the safe. I go upstairs one last time, look at my room, see pail, and towel, and Evian bottle, of course, still on the hallway rug. Downstairs, I reconsider one final time the matter of the envelopes, decide I simply must leave them, anyway estimate that they won't be found before nine-thirty, by which time I hope to have checked in for my flight. I decide not to turn on the outside or entry light, to avoid waking Paddy, in his cottage. I walk with my suitcase and my handbag across the drive. As I lean into the car to put my suitcase in the back, the car key drops out of my hand. I stand, in pitch dark now, and in heavy rain. I begin to search, the driveway, the gravel circle, the adjoining grass, the car. I kneel to look underneath the car, and my corduroy slacks are soaked. I return to the house, turn on, after all, the entry light; but the key dropped on the far side, in the dark shadow of the car. Finally, I find the key, somewhere inside the car itself, calm down, walk back to the doorway, turn off the entry light, roar off. No light at the gateway cottage, no light anywhere, no cars on the road, either, it seems. So I am not being followed. At the airports, of course, there may be someone. Still, though there's sometimes rain, sometimes clouds, sometimes a clear black sky and that sickle moon, I am on my way.

Quanta, Amy said, on the train, in that blizzard, in answer to my question. Not here, Diana said, to her lasting regret, to her own daughter, who approached her, crying, in front of all those people.

The turning point at the paper was the introduction of the byline.

He ceased to be a writer from the moment he began to tape.

The truth was, there was something in the ice cube.

I don't want these colloquies and asides, you know, any more than I want to hear how the reporter got the story. But so much of the story, for some time now, has been, says who?

Grieved like, pined like . . . Why must there always be a simile? Why must you drive always to first questions, way beyond the goalposts every time. Well, what do you keep sacking our quarterback for, when it comes to that.

She had loved him, you know, with the operatic intensity of a basset, or a diva, or a child.

I find the turnoff *to* Castlebar all right. I've seen it on my way to and from the Waltons'. Then I drive straight, straight, and the rain stops, the sky is clear black, all the stars are there. I cannot see, on either side, the roadside, but I have the sense, always, of those long stone walls, meadows, sometimes the sea, the cows, the incredible unseen beauty of the Irish countryside. Only a car or two, at intervals of many minutes. On what errands can they be, on what errand am I, why are cars so few? And in the isolated houses, even in the towns, no lights in any windows, except, again many miles apart, one light, upstairs or down: a solitary insomniac, a worker on the night shift, a terrorist, a poet, who? But in the long spells of driving through the dark, there begins to arise in me an exaltation. I cannot see where this will end. I still have the sense, how to put this, that the land, even the sleeping country towns, know of me. That they are aware that I am passing, whether they follow or not: one car, torn fender, missing rental sticker, bound, they cannot yet know for where. Suddenly, street lights, curves, a traffic light or two. No sign that I can see, however, for Dublin, or any other major town. So I drive straight on, and when the lights and intersections recede, I assume that what I have just been through is downtown metropolitan Castlebar itself, such as it is. Straight on, exhilaration. Is it the hour? the passing over into crime? although I know in my legal heart I cannot yet have broken any law. What comes to me now, as I look up at Orion, and think of childhood knowledge of stars, myths, constellations, dinosaurs, is also the memory, the physical courage of that outlaw, that reckless vandal, fearless of death, that child. Into this kinetic scofflaw joy, the realization that I have, in all probability, missed my turnoff, the turning round, the car arrived too late to see me turn, so that, if he was following, I will have lost him now. And what, I have thought, if I'm caught actually getting on the plane at Dublin. Why, I'll say I was planning to return tomorrow. Ask them at Cihrbradàn, ask also Captain Walton. And my car's not due till then; look, I still have the key here in my pocket. At the airport, I will have bought a ticket to return, tomorrow, from London. Look, I have a ticket back to Ireland. And the missing rental sticker. I have already explained it. (I can't say I don't know how it came off; someone may have seen me remove it.) It's in order not to be over-charged for car repairs. And I would use the argument of so many arguing from the botched nature of their crimes: Would I have done this, kept the key, parked the car with its torn fender facing out, peeled off the sticker, if I was really intending to abscond. Do you take me for such a fool, I mean, what kind of fool do you take me for. But I'm uneasy, uneasy, about what happens after that. Do they say: A likely story. No. But do I have to stay, and pay, right then and there, whatever extortionate price I'm becoming a fugitive to avoid. Almost certainly. I'm uneasy, in fact, about what happens as I get nearer to Dublin. If I am getting nearer to Dublin. And then I notice that the fuel gauge registers only slightly more than a quarter of a tank. I drive on, counting the miles I have driven back from the point where I turned around, wondering how much mile-age I have wasted. What looms behind me, of course, is that im-mense truck. And when I flag him down, he stops. I ask him the way to route N.5 for Dublin, and there crosses his face that look of suspicion, hesitation, which I recognize even by night; I have now so often seen it. He says, I'm going to Dublin, you can follow me. We set out, and then I start to suspect him. My trust, in other words, is entirely depleted, and I wonder whether they have sent another of their agents, or alerted him, and is he headed now, not to Dublin at all, but straight back to the station at Castlebar. There is Kafka's castle, of course, and the castle where I have been staying; and the bar, well, I leave that train of thought. And Mummy's beach. All the time, there persists my own inexplicable impression that there has been something quite wrong in the course of these events, and I keep wondering what it is, apart from a small accident in which I have been at fault, wondering just what it is that they can want to frame me for, in the matter of this car. I think instead of ways to account for the man's hesitation. I think, perhaps he thought I'm IRA, dressed like that, in the night, on whatever errand, in that scarred car, with my corduroy pants, and my down jacket. And then the other thought occurs, perhaps he's IRA, and his truck is loaded with gelignite, and what accounts for his suspicion is that he thinks I am the police. And the sheer unlikelihood of this position, this situation, the sheer statistical implausibility of it, begins once again to strike me, and I am full of joy, only partially diminished by the fact that I am no longer quite alone. Solitude has seemed so much a part of the adventure until now.

The schema is this, a jug band; the schema's a clarinet quintet; the schema's a guitar, a fado, an orchestra. Going with Paul Wiseman on his motorbike to the Boston Symphony; the little girl onstage playing an oboe in Gina's kindergarten class; John's saying, frankly, I think letting women into the Century would be as inappropriate as introducing a trombone into a string quartet.

When I learned about the shrew, the poor unevolved, benighted shrew, which will keep jumping high in the air at a place in its accustomed path where an obstacle, a rock perhaps, once was but no longer is, well, I wondered about all those places where, though the obstacles have long been removed, one persists either in the jump or in taking the long way round. It seemed such an unnecessary jolt or expenditure of time and energy. And yet if you have acquired a profound aversion for just such a place simply because of an obstacle that once was there, or an incapacity to discern that the obstacle no longer exists, or an indifference as to whether it exists or not, or if the habit of pointless jumping, or detour, or even turning back dejected has become for you the path itself, or if you have a superstitious need to treat the spot as though the obstacle remained, or even a belief that the discovery that the obstacle is gone is in itself a punishable offense, if any of these things is true for you, then you are lost. Or probably lost, unless the habitual path, the compulsion, the leap, the turning back, the long detour have for you another value. Individuality, for instance, love, obsession. Or for that matter, art.

Is this the way you lead your life? I said. You said no. I said, me neither. And that delayed it for a year.

The road now is sometimes clear, sometimes overlaid for quite a stretch with mist. On both sides still, of course, in that intense, modulated dark, the incredible, unseen beauty of the Irish country-side. I look at my watch, 4:35, and since I've taken my eyes off the road, and since we are speeding, I think, Will it be said that she died while/because she was looking at her watch? I look at the fuel gauge. I look at the gas stations, every one of which is closed. I pass the truck, on the right of course, and, hazard lights flashing yet again, I wave, full of hope that he will not leave me now, I wave again for him to stop. I say I'm running out of gas. He looks shifty, suspicious, sly. I point to my fuel gauge. I ask whether there will be any gas stations open on the way to Dublin. He says not before nine-thirty. I say, Are there no all-night stations then in Ireland. He says no. I ask how much further it is to Dublin. He says, About a hundred twenty miles. I have not yet learned that distances in Ireland are so notoriously understated that there is an actual distance that the English call an Irish mile. But I say, I'll never make it. My flight from Dublin leaves at ten. And I ask, Can I just drive till I run out of fuel, and then ride the rest of the way with you. And he says, That would be all right. And he speaks softly, and has a stammer; but, as I say, I have grown by now to love him. We drive and drive, and there's a sign reading Bally-haunis 10. I wonder whether my car will make it that far. I wonder if, when I stop, he will just keep going. But we reach a town. He slows down, and so do I. This is evidently Ballyhaunis. Though there is a parking lot, of sorts, in the village square, with several cars parked, and several empty spaces, he suggests that I park my car elsewhere, beside the curb. I ask again, since I may have mis-heard him, whether I should lock the car. He says, Oh yes. So I lock the car. He waits. He opens his door. I hand my bags up to him. Since the cab is very high, and I'll have to be unencumbered to climb on, I also hand him my purse. He shuts his door. I go around to the other side. He leans over and opens that door for me. I manage to climb aboard. I slam the door. I find I am still, for some reason, clutching the rental agency's Irish map. And off we go.

I ask whether my car will be all right, parked at that curb. He says, Yes, no one will notice; these towns are small. There is a long silence. He says, Where have you come from, then? I tell my first lie. I say, Just beyond Castlebar. Another silence. I say, The car belongs to friends, they can come and pick it up when I phone and tell them where it is. A pause. He says, Yes, with another key. I think, He obviously knows I'm lying. Maybe not. I ask where he's from. He says Achill Island. I ask how often he makes this run to Dublin. He says, Two nights a week. I ask what load the truck is carrying. He laughs, says, A little of everything. It occurs to me yet again that he may be as much or as little of an outlaw as I am, that possibility. After a long spell, he asks where I'm from. I say, Boston, Massachusetts. He laughs, says, You are a long way from home, then. I say, Yes, I am. I'm flying to London, to see my brother. He says, Why not: To see your brother. I say, Well, he's just passing through London. A very long silence. He says, Do you work in London, then? I cannot remember whether I have already said anything on this subject, so I say no; and then, improbably, that I may be transferred there. I watch the road, wondering what I shall say is my profession, and how I'll explain what I'm doing here. He doesn't, it seems, understand too well what I say, either, so it occurs to me that, if I'm caught in an inconsistency or a lie, he may think he's simply misunderstood it. I say, I'm on vacation, I was supposed to come early this summer, but I couldn't, I'm here now instead, and since my brother is passing through London, I'm going to see him. Just for the day. A pause. Come to think of it, I say, I don't need to phone my friends. I can pick up the car myself, on the way back. He brightens, begins to tell me, in enormous detail, what sequence of buses I'll need to take to return from Dublin airport to Ballyhaunis. In order to pick up my car. Our longest silence yet. I was going to tell him I work for a computer company, or perhaps a tool manufacturer. Finally, it comes to me. I'm going to say that I work for a religious organization, the World Council of Churches, perhaps, or Joint Church Aid. I am very pleased with this notion.

I may even say that my brother is a priest. We drive and drive in silence, and then I ask him whether he belongs to a union. He says he does. I wonder, though I don't ask, what the union is called. I suppose it isn't teamster. He suddenly begins to complain, at length, that new rules will soon be in force. No hauls more than eight consecutive hours. A compulsory break every four hours. The speed limit for trucks, all over Ireland, thirty-five miles an hour. He says, No lorry driver will keep to it. I ask how they, they are going to catch every lorry driver who breaks the speed limit. The logs, he says, with some indignation; they don't even have to catch you on the road and pull you over. They can get you on the logs. I sympathize with him, particularly about the thirty-five-mile limit, and we are now at one in at least this opposition to the law. He says again that no lorry driver will keep to it. I ask him whether they will strike. I do not understand the particulars of his answer, but I gather that the drift is Yes. (In the matter of logs, I am reminded of the black bus driver, on the route from Red Hill to the Port Authority, and the Connecticut trooper who pulled him over. The little insurrection of the passengers, who thought the trooper was questioning the logs because the bus driver was black. On that other bus, the passenger who took out from his flight bag, and held under his coat, a hammer. His shaven head, his pallor, the hammer in his hand.) More than an hour passes, partly in silence, partly in not understanding each other's conversation. Then he tells a long story about an aunt of his, who came over from the States, near Boston, to see Dublin, and his truck, and the back of it, and its taking a bump, and how she laughed, and what he thought she would say when she got back to the States. I ask how old his aunt is, but this turns out, for some reason, to be an entirely dissonant question. He says, About fifty, and I realize or think he may already have said so. Then I say, You must come to Boston someday, and this seems better, though I still can't understand what he says in answer. I have said very little about the religious organization for which I work, and he has not asked much about it. We are strangely reserved in what we ask each other. It still seems far from inconceivable that his A little of everything back there *is* gelignite. I realize that I am free to make up a lie of any kind, and so is he.

As the miles and the hours pass, I realize that we are not going to ask each other's names, or tell them. He says, So you're going to smoke city. It is the first time I sense even a remote hostility toward England. I say, Yes, we have several missions there. A pause. I ask whether he takes a ferry from Achill Island. He says, There is a bridge. I ask whether the truck is his. He says, I wish it were. He says he has been a member of his union forty years, and that he will never consent to drive only eight hours on the nights he drives. How many hours does he like to drive, usually? I ask. He says, As many as I can. I think of the talk, at the Waltons', about the Irish working man. Point, set, and match. I know I will not be able to offer him money when I leave his truck (he has said he will not drive me into Dublin, but leave me at a bus stop, on the out- skirts, much closer to the airport, where I can catch a bus direct; more about this, in due course, but I believe him, naturally); and I've wondered how I'm going to thank him. Thinking now along the lines of my profession, I know I'm going to say: I hope we meet again and that I can do him a favor someday; but also, especially, God bless you. He asks why I don't take a little time off, this morn- ing, and have a look at Dublin. I say, But I would miss my flight, and miss seeing my brother. A long silence. He asks something about my friends beyond Castlebar, and my answer makes no sense even to me. As we approach Dublin, and the sun is just rising at the outskirts, he talks about the time it would take to drive me to the airport, direct, in all that traffic. And there does start to be a lot of traffic. At last, he drops me at a bus shelter. He hands me down my bags. I say thank you. I add, God bless you. He drives off.

There are three young people standing in that bus shelter. I ask, Do all the buses from here go to the airport? And with that obdurateness, satisfaction, even mockery, they say, These buses don't go to the airport. You'll have to go into Dublin for a bus to get there; it's the other way. And they exchange looks. I am a little stunned by this. I say, Shall I catch a bus from here to Dublin, then? And they say, That's what you'll have to do. One of the girls adds, If they're not full. She starts to flag down a bus, which is just coming. It doesn't stop, and she says, with great satisfaction, That one's full. We wait. I see, by some miracle, a black car that appears to be a taxi, coming from the direction the lorry driver and I have come from. I say, I guess I'd better try and get a cab then, and wave to him. By another miracle, he pulls over and he has no passenger. I ask how much it will be to the airport. He says six or seven pounds. It barely crosses my mind to wonder whether the truck driver can have been mistaken, about the direction of the airport, about the itinerary of the buses; to wonder also why he did not take me, at least, into Dublin. But he is, by then, still so much my friend that I just have to assume it was a mistake of some sort, and perhaps it was. I don't believe it was. But, whatever his errand or intention may have been, he stopped for me. He didn't have to. It prolonged his work day. Work night. He stopped for me. And whatever he may have thought my errand was, well, how else can I put it? I feel warmly toward him still. The fact, however, is that had it not been for that providential, empty cab, I would almost certainly, no, certainly, have missed my plane.

The cab driver says, What time's your flight? I say, Ten, but I ought to be there by nine-fifteen. I still have to get my ticket and check in. He says, Well, in this traffic, I'd better take you through the park. Where've you been staying, then? I say, Just outside of Dublin. A pause. Several minutes pass. I say, Is this way much longer. He says, No, actually it's shorter. This is clearly untrue, else why would he have said we'll go through the park, on account of traffic, in the first place. Also, we seem to have run into more traffic than he had expected. He becomes impatient. I say, The park is lovely. He says nothing. I think I ought to ask some sort of question. If I've been staying just outside of Dublin, of course, I don't know what kind of question I would ask. (I suddenly remember a moment with the lorry driver: as we neared Dublin, and the sun was just rising at the outskirts, and it was clear that the time and distance were much longer than I had expected, I realized that I wouldn't be able to deliver my car at any airport, having left it behind, of course, at Ballyhaunis. Also, that my argument that I planned to pick up that car tomorrow was pretty weak. How, then, explain that, having left a damaged car, in an obscure town, by night, I leave Ireland now, intending, all the same, to return the car to its rental agency by Friday afternoon. A problem, certainly. But I had my new, my religious identity, and suddenly it dawned on me: what I was going to do was to fly out of Ireland under another name. In order not to get caught at this, I would not use my credit card; I would use cash. And I would have to inquire, too, whether one has to show one's passport, in leaving or in entering Ireland. As I recalled, one did not have to show it. I could pretend I was asking on behalf of someone else. My boss, perhaps, or my brother. If passports were required, I would of course have to risk my own name. Otherwise, I would just pay in cash, under whatever name, and leave. Traveling under a false name might be a crime of some sort. I should make the name as like my own as possible to account for the mistake. Alder, I thought. But then that does happen so often. I was afraid they might make the same mistake and be on the lookout for just such an Alder. So I thought, Hadley, since no one would look under H. And then, in my new hilarity, I thought, Why not Haddock. But that seemed going too far. So I settled, now, on Hadley.) At the airport, the meter registers nine pounds, and of course he had said six or seven. I have a sense now of his feeling somewhat contrite, or perhaps only abashed. But I am not thinking of it. I pay him ten pounds fifty. He stops, turns around, and says, It's too much. I say, What do you mean? He says, The fare's only nine pounds. I say, I know, I just wanted you to have something. And he says, God bless you.

Well, the answer to my question, whether one needs to show one's passport, was no. Then, I asked the agent at the ticket counter whether I could pay in mixed currencies. She said, No, only one. I wanted to make it short. So I thought, What the hell, and gave her my credit card. She saw the discrepancy in names, and said, Oh, I've got it wrong. I said, No, the name on my credit card's my maiden name, It's a name I sometimes use. And there, of course, was the argument, Do you take me for such a fool as to use my card, and to say I've got two names. Then, she said, my computer doesn't check out the card. I said, What does that mean, do you call them, or what. She said, Do you want me to call them? I said yes. Then it was all right, and she said, Sorry for the delay. I said, I was worried for a minute there. She said, No, sometimes the computer does that; what's really embarrassing though is when I call them, and they say it's stolen or in arrears, and they ask me not to give it back. The ticket bought, I went upstairs. Then, the news that the British Airways flight would be late, first ten minutes, then twenty. Hungry now for breakfast, I hesitated at the bar, in the departure lounge. As I counted pence, looking for change to buy some biscuits, a man who stood drinking at the bar turned to me and said, Are you a writer? My heart sank. I said, Does it show. He said, I can tell. This time, something akin, in retrospect, to the argument from What kind of fool occurred to me on *their* behalf. If they, they were following me, if that man was an agent, would they be such fools, would he be such a fool, as to alert me, to warn me, by addressing to me a question that could only fill me with suspicion and alarm. Well, yes they might, for several reasons: spontaneously, or as a check on my spontaneous reaction to being identified; a ploy to get me to do something, or refrain from doing it. I lurked outside the bar, in the departure lounge a bit, studying that drinking man, wondering whether he was really drinking at this early hour, or just posing as an Irish alcoholic. Security, in these times, would surely require agents at all Irish airports, watching for bombs, guns, fugitives, aliases, God knows what. Perhaps they could not be bothered with mere tortfeasors like myself. Not wanting to lurk, however, I walked to a row of chairs, just outside the barred corridor to the chute beyond which there ought to be a plane. There was no plane. Another announcement, saying the flight would be ten minutes later than previously announced. I began to wonder whether I would not do better, after all, on Aer Lingus, whose scheduled departure was now a mere fifteen minutes after the announced time for British Airways. I asked, at the last-minute check-in counter, whether the Aer Lingus flight, which I could plainly see outside, might leave on time and first. The ticket agent, or whatever he was, said, It won't. So I sat down. I decided to go to the ladies' room, but there was a row of chairs in front of it, with a board over them, and a sign saying Out of Order. I walked by the men's room. I saw a door marked with a sign depicting a little man in a wheelchair. I went in. There, with the door half open, was a woman, sitting on the toilet and holding the hand of a small child. I waited outside the door, till they came out. Since the toilet had not been flushed, I thought it was out of order. But, when

I pulled the handle, it flushed readily. I went back, resumed my chair in the departure lounge, nearer the chute, and unfolded one of my newspapers.

I looked up; and just beyond the agent's booth, I saw two men in conversation. One, fat, dark-haired, pale, wearing a rounded collar, tie, sweater, and jacket, and carrying a raincoat, faced in my direction. The other, sandy-haired, wearing a brown suit, also carrying a trenchcoat, faced the other way. I left, through the steel maze, and walked around the men. I began to imagine that the man who had his back to me was the one I had seen drinking in the bar. I went back to the bar to look. He was no longer there. The sandy-haired man, near the booth, had a beard, which I had not previously noticed, or had I? When I passed in the direction he was facing, it seemed to me he turned away. I went back to my seat. I thought, What was my crime so far; none that I could see, except traveling under an alias, which I had not yet done. I got up, and said to the British Airways ticket agent, or whatever he was, that I'd like to change the name on my ticket. To make it proper for my records. He said his was only the last-minute check-in. To change, I would have to go back to the downstairs ticket counter. And there wasn't time for that. I said, In that case I'll have to take Aer Lingus. He said, That's up to you. Having established, now, my good intentions, and my what kind of fool do you take me for, regarding the false name, I looked at the two men, still engaged in conversation. The sandy-haired one had been joined now by a woman. I thought I'd wait to see whether they entered the area inside the chute. I could, after all, always leave at the last minute. They seemed, all three of them, to be staring at me now. When I sat in another place, to face the sandy-haired man, he and his girl turned. So did the dark, fat man, so that he again faced me, in his round collar, dark tie, maroon sweater, and the sandy-haired one again had his back to me. When I left again, through the steel maze, they exchanged words, then entered the area beside the chute and sat down. I thought, Will they board the plane and fly away if I do not board it. Not a chance. So we'll have the same episode or sequence, if I change to the Aer Lingus flight. But what if I outwait them, they get on the flight, that is, and I don't. They'd get off. So I thought, Might as well get it over with, but still I waited. Then they boarded all passengers bearing green boarding passes. That's what I had, a green boarding pass. But I waited and waited. I could see two of their boarding passes were brown. Finally the dark, fat man got up. He had a green boarding pass, and used it. I used mine, and I followed him, but lurked, lingered in the boarding chute. I started back, thinking I might say I'd taken fright. But I wavered, havered, went back, looked at him to see if he had turned to look at me, then thought, What the hell, and got on. The couple, the sandy-haired, bearded man and the girl, got on. I was seated right behind the dark, fat man. They were seated in the smoking section, several rows behind me. I thought, Now would surely be the time to arrest me, if they were going to do it. Perhaps they could have done so, when my boarding pass was taken. Would they surround me, and walk me off the flight, then? But they did nothing. And, even in my state, I knew they could hardly arrest me in the air.

Quanta, Amy said to me, on the train, in that blizzard, in answer to my question. Not here, Diana said, to her lasting regret, to her own daughter, who approached her, crying, in front of all those people. Not here. But in London, don't you see, the phone rang. In London, the phone calls began.

Well, I waited. I told no one. For the next few days, in any case, my voice was gone; it might have been a fever. I waited for them to find the car. I waited for them to find the ticket, me. But it was not until long afterward, when it was explained to me, that I understood that there was, after all, something else quite wrong in the course of these events, and that there really was something they were trying to frame me for, in the matter of the car. But I didn't understand it then. Quanta. Not here.

You can see it from here; but just try to get to it.

But do you sometimes wish it was me? Always. Pause. It is you.

III. HOME

But in London, don't you see, the phone rang. The phone calls began. I was asleep. He said, You've left, I said, Well, no.

It is only a small house, though it is old, on an acre-and-a-half of land. It is screened from the road by a grey, weathered eight-foot fence and an uneven row of ragged pines. All the acres that surround the property are owned by a neurotic Lebanese, but the house, which is red with white trim, used to be a cider mill. It overlooks a waterfall, a brook, and two small ponds. The upper pond is shallow. The man from whom I bought the place said he used to skate, with his little granddaughter, on that pond, a distance, I think, of maybe thirty gliding steps around. The lower pond is deep, and he said he used to swim in there. Room for just a few strokes, virtually in place. The upper pond, which has a sudden, jagged bend on one side, is lined in summer with rushes, covered in the fall with leaves. The roof of the front porch of the house is covered, for some reason, with moss, and also, on one side, with wisteria, which gives the house a sort of raffish Veronica Lake look, a disheveled charm. In fact, the whole place is quaint, so quaint that it sometimes seems quite magical. Why, you could put an island with bridges in that little pond, the great professor, who advised governments from Lima to Baghdad on land use, said when he came to visit, and have something perfect, enchanted, Japanese. It's a jewelry box, my Aunt Zabeth said, the first time she saw it. At other times, the quaintness can seem a little sick. There is also, oddly, an enormous flagpole, taller than the one in town on Main Street, which loomed high over the house, and which, together with the upper pond, somehow created the impression of a hazard near a golfing green. I could never remove a flagpole. I still have an American flag, with forty-eight stars, which was given to me by a Japanese boy called Junior, when we were in kindergarten. Soon after I moved in, I simply asked Paul, the neighborhood handyman, how much it would cost to move the flagpole, away from the house and the pond, toward some trees near the corner of the property. He said several hundred dollars. Then I asked how much it would take to change the shape of the upper pond, make it narrower and deeper, less like a golf hazard and more clear. Four thousand dollars, he said, at the very least. And there was always the danger that the house would be flooded, or even borne away, in spring.

So I did nothing. For three years, I neglected the place, only having the small patch of lawn beside the path mowed by an old man who said he had always mowed it. But the man from whom I bought the place had told me that the upper pond needed to be dredged every few years, when it filled up with silt. Late one summer, when there had been a dry spell, the waterfall was silent, the lower pond was nearly empty, and the upper pond so full of silt, rushes, maybe reptiles that, when its four surprising ducks had gone, it became a source mainly of mosquitoes. I looked in the yellow pages. Found contractor. Found excavating contractor, Lucas Scott, on a road four miles away. It was Sunday. I called him. He arrived within the hour. He said virtually nothing, but his estimate was low; I really liked him. Two days later, there was Sidney, a Korean veteran I thought, though I never asked, driving the enormous backhoe. Arrived late in the afternoon, churning up whatever there had ever been of lawn, making smithereens of flagstones. Parked that huge, thundering, ringing machine, with its hand (as the hands of those machines are always parked at night) knuckles to the ground. Oiled it. Left it there overnight. The elbow of it towering over my house against the moonlight. The next day, Sid was dredging silt, tons and tons of silt, and placing it behind a line of enormous boulders; twelve huge trucks arrived all day and dumped those boulders, shaking the earth for miles around. Sid placed them in a line, where I asked him to, with that great, heavy, precise, iron hand. I had no notion what an immense thing it is to change the contours of even the smallest pond, or for that matter to divert a flow of water. Neighbors I never knew came, while the machine thundered, and its safety device clanged warnings, and the boulders shook the earth. Neighbors came to watch, and to make remarks, also dire predictions. When the first day was over, the machine looming in the dark again at rest, I saw the silt, the line of rocks, a still unplaced heap of boulders, the flagpole which the machine had plucked like a daisy and replanted elsewhere. Sludge. And I thought, If this is the externalization of a psychological state, I am in more trouble than I ever knew.

Let me just say that I
No.
What do you mean, No? Let me just
No.
No?
No. I'm tired of it already. I don't want to hear about it. I don't want to see it. I don't want to tell it. I want no part of it at all.
Well then what
Just leave me alone.
Well, then I can't
Don't apologize. Just let it pass.
But I.
Go away.

On the plane, when I last went away, the movie had long flickered out, those passengers with whole rows to themselves were sound asleep, others sat, staring, with their blankets and their little earphones. The man a seat away from me bought me a drink, gave

me his card, and said that, though he had been a year too young
for the Korean conflict, he was the third member of his family to
have served in the Marines. His grandfather had been an only son,
so had his father, so was he. All had been Marines, until they came
home, married, and entered the family business—factories that
made metal containers, cans. Did I favor an all-volunteer Army?
he suddenly asked. I hesitated, then said No, I preferred the draft,
it seemed more fair. Well, he said, ordering another drink, he had
just spent days with procurement officers at the Pentagon. They
wanted him to devise a can for what used to be called A rations, a
container such that when rations were dropped from airplanes to
ground troops there would be no breaking or crumbling of Saltines.
It was impossible, he said, his factory simply could not do it.
Must there be Saltines? I asked. Yes, he said. An all-volunteer
Army has its culinary demands. On the way back, another man in
his mid-forties asked me whether I would mind watching his hatbox. We were at Heathrow. I had not seen a hatbox since I was
a child. He said he was bringing a hat as a present to his wife, but
that there were also heavy objects in the hatbox. He wanted to run
over and say goodbye to his father. He and his father, he said, never
took the same flight. Family policy or company policy? I asked. He
had given me his card by then. It showed him as treasurer, his
father as president of a conglomerate. Company policy, he said.
Then, while I, against all my resolutions, ate the awful airline
lunch, and he drank, without any visible effect, six vodkas, he told
me that he too had been a Marine, and that his wife was a private
detective. The wife the hat was for. His grandfather, he said, had
invented many things, including the x-ray equipment with which
the family company began. One morning, many years ago, a distinguished surgeon had been discussing with this grandfather the
problem of tuberculosis and the poor. Was there not some way, the
surgeon wondered, to make chest x-rays inexpensive and also, since
it was often difficult to persuade uneducated people to go to hospitals for examinations, to make the x-rays available to the poor in
their own neighborhoods? The grandfather, who was already rich in
those days, not only invented equipment for inexpensive x-rays; he
made it mobile, and sent it, on wheels, to all the city's neighborhoods. In all the decades since then, his company had provided the

x-rays free. On a summer evening, a few years ago, one of the x-ray wagons was hijacked by a group of Puerto Rican radicals, the F.A.L.N. Let me say, this isn't a matter of how I see things. This is what actually happens: going over Saltines and the all-volunteer Army, coming back x-ray wagons hijacked by the F.A.L.N. And the thing of course is this, that to me my life is serious. It is just that, I don't know, the reality I inhabit is already slant. In the sense I think that Emily Dickinson meant by Tell it true but tell it slant.

Not here, Diana said. This is about friendship, and my tantrum, and how I both was and failed to be a citizen of my time. One would never have guessed they were a couple. She seemed so much older, of no clear age, but of another generation, it seemed certain, than he was. She was dark, heavy, in some way altogether ancient beautiful, by birth and accent Greek. He was slight, slim, boyish, by accent and manner unmistakably New England; well-traveled, though, bright, worldly, wearing his parka, over sweater, tennis shoes, and jeans, against the wind. One would have thought him, at the very oldest, twenty-eight. When it turned out, hours after the first introductions, incompletely understood, that they were, in fact, a couple, John and Diana Cummings, it turned out as well that he was, must be, from his first accounts of his life and education, forty-five, and she, it became clear, could be no more than ten years older. Even then, they seemed so oddly matched, so unmatched, that one thought they must have met and married only recently. He, seeking in his boyishness a mother, perhaps, or a guardian. She, seeking a son perhaps to look after and protect. They had, in fact, been married more than twenty years. They had two daughters; also, a son, of whom they rarely spoke. Here's what happened on the first evening, at dinner. Somebody asked me what I was working on. I said, A piece about the American passport. Ah yes, said the Austrian photographer, a good subject. And she told of her travails in being admitted to the United States. She was asked, of course, whether she had been a Communist, but also whether she had ever committed adultery. What a question, she said. If I were a Communist or an adulteress, did they think I would say yes? I spoke of the belief I had been brought up with, the particular trust and belief in the American passport. And of how incomprehensible it was to me that any person, government, or bureau should treat it lightly or foolishly, in the matter of regulation, or in any other matter at all. I mentioned that I keep, that my family have always kept, constantly renewed and valid passports. Then it struck me, briefly, vaguely, that, in the matter of trusting and not trusting one's country, a constantly renewed passport cuts both ways. But by this time, Diana had mentioned her own passport, her Greek passport, which had been revoked on account of her activity abroad against the junta. She had, nonetheless, managed, with courage and with an anomalous French passport, to keep traveling, in and out of Greece, but also, once, to Turkey. I asked her about her colleague, the Portuguese feminist and journalist, who had just published a short novel about her lover, an Armenian poet, who died in a Greek prison. And Diana said, Yes, we wanted her to write about another prisoner, but Maddalena insisted it be he. Then, she laughed. In those days, she said, we still believed in publicity, that it matters. She laughed again. I said, What do you mean? What do you now think matters? And she said, Violence.

The passport, I had noticed, was growing smaller, over the years, and changing fabric. I had learned from the dragon of the passport office that they even planned to diminish it, within a year or two, to the size and texture of a credit card. To avoid fraud, they said, but also, and there seemed to me an unconscious totalitarian longing in this, to serve, as papers required on one's person in police states have always served, as permanent proof of citizenship, and of identity.

But in London, don't you see, the phone rang. In London, on Hays Mews in fact, the phone rang. I was asleep. He said, You've left. I said, I haven't. He said, You have.

But will they understand it if I tell it this way?

Yes, they will. They will surely understand it.

But will they care about it?

That I cannot guarantee.

I said, What do you mean? What do you now think matters? And she said, Violence. Diana had also said, The only ones who helped us in those days were the Palestinians. But we had just met, and I didn't even know who "us" was or what, helped with what, so I let it pass. And then, when only she and John and I were still at the table, she said, I understand everything about Greek drama now. And she told of having asked an old Greek in a little mountain village whether he had ever heard of Diana; she meant the goddess. He had replied: I never met her, but she was very beautiful; my grandfather knew her very well. Then she said, What I understand about Greek tragedy now is this: the Athenians went to three dramas in a single day, and at the end they were so exhausted, that was the catharsis. The exhaustion itself was the catharsis. She and John and their daughter had gone, it seems, to a therapy group, in Lausanne, where they live. And the daughter had gotten up, one of the first to speak, and said many things about her parents. John had gotten up to answer, doing so quietly, in his way and so as not to hurt his daughter, and crying as he spoke, which is not at all his way or the way of that sort of American. Then, it was Diana's turn. She had looked around, she said, and thought, These worms, I can do this easily, these worms, particularly as I have been through a lot in my life, and now I am going to act, that is perform. But somewhere in the course of her speaking she was moved to tears, and when she had finished, the leader, knowing that this marked an emotional caesura for the whole group, called an intermission. And during the intermission the gathering broke as it were into three large factions, some with John, some with Diana, but a great wave bearing her daughter toward Diana, wanting reconciliation, a scene. Diana thought again, These worms. And, as her daughter was borne directly to her, crying, Diana said, "Not here." But this is not about that. In the end, this is not about that, though that "Not here" had immense repercussions for me. This is about friendship, and my tantrum, and how I both was and failed to be a citizen of my time.

These are the categories: arbitrary, necessary, futile. Intimate, public. These are the characters, these are the events. Over here, are the strategies and theories. Cadences. And in London, after all, there were the phone calls. Sometimes I was asleep, sometimes you were.

This is a conservative, even a reactionary town, and yet, every year since anyone can remember, it has been the only town in the state to have a Labor Day parade. Frank and Marilyn, my nearest neighbors, are conservative, even reactionary voters. We became friends in the first week I moved here. Marilyn brought a flowering plant in welcome, stayed for coffee and a cigarette, then called to ask whether I would like to come to dinner the following night at five o'clock. Five o'clock, I thought, farmers' hours, country people's hours, although our farming neighbors, when I was growing up, I dimly recalled, had dinner more nearly at six or even six-thirty, and though I knew that Frank and Marilyn are not farming people. She runs a private kindergarten; he is an engineer. When I arrived at their house, there was for some time no question at all of eating. They were already drinking, and I joined them. When we did finally have dinner, hamburgers, I think, with spaghetti sauce and wine, it was long after eleven. And by the time I crossed the road, through the chill air, to my house, we had told each other more than some close friends of many years. Just as well. Our driveways are close enough for us to see who comes and goes, and, from time to time, hear bits of conversation, borne with improbable clarity on the night wind. What we would have known anyway, as neighbors, we know instead as friends. They are kind, educated, tolerant, church-going people, with their own history of trouble, bordering at one time on local scandal; and when I mention what I think of as their conservatism, quite apart from how they vote, I mean, for instance this: at odd hours, motorcycles and heavy trucks have begun of late to thunder at high speeds along our road, using it as a short cut between one highway and another. Apart from the noise, this back road, which is narrow and winding, was not meant for speed, or for the weight and width of trucks. In winter, especially, there are always crashes. When some neighbors suggested a petition, to post signs lowering the speed limit and also reading No Thru Trucks, Frank and Marilyn refused to sign. They so disliked the Sierra Club, Clamshell Alliance overtone, they said. This position carried in our neighborhood. All winter there will again, presumably, be crashes. But Frank says it is clear, at least, that this is not and will never be a Clamshell Alliance sort of town.

As a child, like many children, I sometimes received a diary with a little lock and key. Each time, and it cannot have been more than five times in all, I would begin, full of hope, on the first page, and immediately become dissatisfied. Not, certainly, on literary grounds. I never got that far. But on grounds (and this still seems odd to me) of penmanship. The thing did not look right. There was always some sort of blot or crooked line. I would try to erase, begin again, then give it up. This object, with its blurred start and months of empty pages, would lie around, be submerged under other books and papers, resurface, finally be thrown out. Only twice in my life have I come any nearer to the keeping of a journal. The second time was in my twenties. In an ordinary notebook, with no lock of course and with undated pages, I wrote daily, from one Sunday to Wednesday of the following week. I don't know which month or year, although I remember that the time was summer. I know the weekdays only because I wrote them, in ballpoint, printed capitals, at the top of every page. What brought the effort to an end on Thursday was that I looked back. I read the entries for the past nine days, and I simply could not understand them. They might have been by a stranger and in code.

The penmanship was fine, still those clear, regular capitals. But the record was of moods. There were no events, few names, no facts, no indication whatever of what *happened*, apart from this gloom, that cheering up, this gloom again. What few names there were appeared uncharacterized, and not part of any incident or sentence; and the moods were described only to the extent of being up or down, like a chart of the stock market or of an illness. There was less information than one would record, in advance, on any social calendar. The events simply were not there, and, more surprisingly, I could not reconstruct them. Not from the mood clues, not from the fact that they had occurred so recently. I could more accurately recall events that had occurred long years before. And the first, the only other time, I tried to keep a journal had, in fact, occurred long years ago, when I was twelve. That journal covered months, on a daily basis, and in very considerable detail. And the salient point about it was only this: that it was lies. My letters, too, at that time and after, consisted largely of what I wanted other people to believe. I wanted that diary found. I cannot believe I was entirely different in this from others. And so, when I read biographies reconstructed largely from diaries, or from letters to, from, or about obscure or famous men and women, it seems to me that unless mine is an isolated and unusual case (and of course, in a way, what is at issue is precisely the class of isolated and unusual cases) those diaries, letters, interesting though they may be, are probably quite largely false. And, as for journals, these days, "I can show you in my journal; I have it right here in my journal" usually implies a threat, by someone who either keeps no journal, or who makes the "it" recorded in it up.

Well, I couldn't go back to sleep, of course, how could I. I said, Of course, I haven't left. He said, You have.

To begin with, I almost went, instead, to Graham Island. I had been muttering for months that I wanted to go somewhere, somewhere else, beautiful and quiet, on the sea. When I went to Jon and Maria's house for dinner, Gavin and Jon, or rather Gavin's wife and Jon had had a quarrel so bitter that Gavin and Jon were going to dissolve their partnership. When I arrived for dinner, Maria was in the kitchen. Gavin and Jon were in the living room. In the tension of their silence, I mentioned wanting to go somewhere, somewhere beautiful and quiet, on the sea. Gavin said he had friends who had a place on an island off Vancouver. Maybe I would like to rent it. I said, How wonderful, and really thought no more about it. The next morning, though, Gavin called and said that the house was in fact available. I could have it, starting next week, for no rent. I said, Oh, I couldn't do that, I absolutely must pay rent. Gavin said, Well, you'll have to discuss that with the owners. So, when I called the owners, I began by saying I really must pay rent. And the assumption was thus, before we even began, that I was going to take the house. The house of strangers, friends of a man I hardly knew, who was about to become a former partner of my friend. They were both on the line, when I called, the owners of this house, husband and wife. They were anthropologists, bright, enthusiastic, kind. The house was on both a river and the sea. One could step out of the house and fish. I was welcome to use their poles.

The island had a rain forest. One flew to Vancouver, from there to another island, then took the ferry; two islands later, there one was. No worry about hospitals, there was a military installation there of sorts, the nearest observation post for Siberia. Siberia, I said. Well, yes, the island was six hundred miles, in fact, from Vancouver. There was a car there, I should pick it up from their friend the Danish baron. Not to worry if, on my way back, my luggage was searched intensively by customs. A weed much sought after by hippies grew there in profusion. The phone, the toaster, and a few other objects of value in the house were concealed, inside a hollow beam. I would find them easily. They were hidden only so that no hippie or other passerby, seeing the phone for instance, would be tempted to make long-distance calls. As soon as I had found the phone, and plugged the jack into the outlet, I should call the owners, and tell them how I was. Also, before leaving for Vancouver, I should call the Danish baron and tell him when I would arrive, so that he could arrange for someone to meet me. At the dock, of the third island by ferry, from the other island, six hundred miles, by air, from Vancouver.

Well, I called the Danish baron, and his accent seemed instantly recognizable to me. I thought, What is this German pretending to be a Dane doing on an American island, six hundred miles from Vancouver, which is the nearest outpost to Siberia. I thought, a war criminal. My state of mind. I still resolved to go. It was somewhere else, somewhere beautiful and quiet, on the sea. Two nights before I left, however, I had a thought. I had begun to worry a bit about the isolation. I called the owners of the house. I reached the wife. How far, I asked, how far from their house was the nearest neighboring house. Oh, she said, not far. You can see it from the window. It's just up the hill actually. A very interesting house. Built and owned by an Indian. A Haida. Of course, he leases it now. The first trace of a hesitation in her voice. To the government of Canada. She distinctly paused. As a retreat. I said, A retreat. She said, Yes. But there are never more than six. I did not ask six what. She said, Alcoholic. Indians. Well, I couldn't do it. Maybe I should have done it, but I couldn't. I still had my ticket to Seattle, though, and somehow that became fixed in my mind. So I called Ted, who had lived, years ago, in Tacoma, and who had bought a house there so remote that even the people who built it for the sake of its remoteness found it too remote and sold it, to ask him where to stay outside Seattle. But it was Friday, he was not in his office. I asked his secretary where he stayed when he was in Seattle. She said, You wouldn't want to stay there, let me find a place where you should stay. I said no, thank you. Within minutes, there was a call from a vice president of Ted's company in Tacoma. He said, We're very hospitable out here. Just tell me what sort of thing you want. I said, Somewhere else, somewhere beautiful and quiet, on the sea. Here's exactly what you do, he said: take the flight to Seattle; at the airport, rent a car, drive to Anacostia, take the ferry. The third stop is Orcas Island. Get off there, drive fifteen miles, to Warriloway, and stay there. So, I did it. And Warriloway turned out to be, among other things, a business conference center, with walls so thin I could hear the man in the next room saying, Sweetie, where did you get these plums, they're really good. She told him, so I drove the thirteen miles and bought plums. At night, I could hear the rock cassettes, by which they went to sleep; and, in the room on the other side, a television set. I was too tired to turn back. The island was as beautiful as any I had ever seen. Here's who else was there: Thelma, the theosophist, who sings songs from *The Sound of Music*, in her operatic voice, so loudly that when she weeds her garden, her voice carries for miles across the bay. Also—her nephew told me this, and I was later able to confirm it—the knobs on the chest of drawers in her bedroom are made of her children's baby teeth. Her husband is a giant, and Thelma and the two daughters I met are also giantesses. At the party of an architect on a mountain top, Thelma mentioned that the Orcas Island camp was the oldest American camp of theosophy. Though I couldn't really remember what theosophy was, I replied with some enthusiasm. She said they had lectures there each day. Some instinct made me ask whether she went to all of them. And she said, Whenever I can. So we were friends. The others I met were the architect, a young tycoon who led a religious cult, and who had had a falling out with a prophet, the founder of it. All the architect's land was nonetheless tax free, being owned by the religious foundation. All the work on his property was free as well, since the young people who worked for him were members of the cult, which obliged them to be in effect his slaves. And his wife, who had been married several times before, once to a college president, was the daughter of one of the major inventors in the early days of NASA. And my other friends, my new friends, there, were a couple, owners of the bookshop, which sold prints. He had been a lawyer, but retired, after his heart attacks, to Orcas Island. His wife, the former lawyer's wife, told me, at the party of the architect on the mountain top, that their daughter, the bookshop owners' daughter, was on her honeymoon. Rowing. From Seattle to Anchorage. A distance of several thousand miles. This daughter and her new husband liked to row. When they first met, they had rowed all the way around Vancouver, a few hundred miles. I asked where, on this longer trip, they spent the nights. She said camped ashore. I asked whether she worried, on their behalf, about Alaskan wolves. Not wolves so much, she said, bears. I asked whether they rowed facing each other, those thousands of miles. She said no. Yet here I am, for the first time and yet again, alone at last on Orcas Island. And yet, this is not entirely the Wasteland; there are so many other people here.

And, in London, after all, there were the phone calls. Sometimes he was asleep. Sometimes I was. He said, You've left. It was my third trip, that fall and winter, standby, New York/London. I said, I haven't. He said, You have. For no reason, and without warning, you've left me, and I'm devastated.

There exists an order of social problem that appears to be insoluble, but is not. At least not in the terms in which resolution of it is represented as impossible. A problem of that sort has at least some of the following features: it appears immensely complicated, with a resolution of any part of it seeming to bring about the aggravation of another; it has a long history, in the course of which it seems to grow, to accrete difficulties, and to merge and overlap with other problems, so that an attempt to solve the single problem appears hopeless without an assault (for which no sufficient resources can exist) upon them all; perception of the length and

nature of that history must be inaccurate, and the terms in which
it has been defined must be so imprecise (or so precise, but inappo-
site) that any formulation of the problem leads inevitably to argument, and great energy is dissipated in argument of that sort.
Ideally, in other words, in its historical dimension, such a problem
appears to have existed forever; and in its contemporary manifesta-
tion to be inextricable from every other problem in the world.
Ideally, too, there should have grown up, over time, a number of
industries and professions nominally dedicated to the eradication
of the problem but actually committed, consciously or uncon-
sciously, but almost inevitably out of self-interest, to the perpetua-
tion of the problem, and of any misconceptions of it, for all time.
Wait a minute. Whose voice is this? Not mine. Not mine. Not
mine. In the matter of problems that appear to be, but are not,
insoluble, the class is the class of all those who profit from a social
blunder. The class does not want to be laid off. Wait. Wait.

In London, I said, But can we live this way.

Quanta. Well, but I, don't you see, I had just taken the shuttle
from Boston to La Guardia, the ordinary shuttle. There was a blizzard, but we took off. When we had been flying for about an hour,
the pilot said, Sorry, folks, there'll be a delay of about twenty minutes; the runway's closed. So we circled La Guardia a long time,
waiting for them to clear the runway, and finally turned back. In
Boston, we all ran through the snow for cabs to the railroad station.
The rumor passed among us that another shuttle, from Washington
to La Guardia, in that blizzard, crashed. Then we heard that the
plane that crashed was not a shuttle. I had settled, though, in my
seat on the train, with my little suitcase, and some Scotch, and
three bags of potato chips that I'd bought with what remained of
my cash, from the bar car. I had settled, wondering how long the
train would take. A couple came toward me. The woman was Amy,
whom I had not seen since she married the man her parents preferred. I knew she had been divorced, not many years later; that
she had two children; that she had become a college professor. I
knew her parents, and the boy with whom she had been in love
when we were children. She introduced the man she was with. She

said they were going to spend the semester break in Guatemala. They had been on the same shuttle flight as I. When she came back from their seats to talk for a while in the seat beside me, she said she had met the man she was with at a college where she used to teach, and where he was the dean. Then we talked for a long time. The blizzard outside was the most dense I remembered, and the train was several times delayed. After a while, I said, Amy, how has it been in your life with unhappiness, did it come in days, months, decades, years? Softly but without hesitation, she said, Quanta. Quanta. There were all the intervening years, and the professorship. There was the dean. Quanta. Not here. She had loved him with the operatic intensity of a basset. Or a diva. Or a child.

Here's what I think is wrong with boring people to no purpose. It's not just that it corrupts their attention, makes them less capable, in other words, of being patient with important things that require a tolerance, to some greater purpose, of some boring time. The real danger lies, I think, in this: that boredom has intimately to do with power. One has only to think of hypnosis, of being mesmerized. Monotony, as a literal method of enthrallment. So this claim to find art in boredom, for its own sake or as one of the modes of alienation, is not simply a harmless misunderstanding, which finds it avant garde to stupefy. Deliberate, pointless boredom is a kind of menace, and a disturbing exercise of power. Of course, that is not always our problem here.

I said, But it's you who always leave. You've just come back from your island. And next week, you'll go again. And anyway. He said, Those are just excuses. The fact is, You've left. I said, I could never really leave.

But, in London, after all, there were the phone calls. And after that. And in the matter of the Irish thing.

This is about the Chinese hypnotist. Here is exactly how it was. I had gone back, after all these years, to the university, and I had six papers due, that last year, near the end. So did all the other students, so I guess have all students since the sixties; but they were going to do them in the end, and I was not. I had, I might as well mention this, a long history of not doing papers. In my first year of college, we all had to do a paper every week. After the first few weeks, I didn't do them, couldn't do them. There were no dropouts, though, in those days, I think. When, at the end of the spring term, the dean said, Miss Ennis, the college requires papers; I suggest, in fact I must insist that you see a psychiatrist this summer. I did. I took a train from Red Hill, where my parents lived, and arrived, two hours later, with a change of trains, in New York. I walked to the office of a tall, pale man, who swept the doily of the previous patient off the couch, replaced it with a relatively fresh one, and said, Well, Miss Ennis, what have we been thinking and feeling. After a week of this, one of my brothers said, This is absurd, you can't keep taking the train to see that fool, this is August, it's too hot. And he wrote my papers. My brother, I mean, wrote my papers. Let me say that I know of few instances where someone has been rescued from something in quite this way. But there it was. More than twenty papers, the weekly ones and the long term papers for other courses. My brother wrote them all. And then, of course, I realized that they were not exactly right; he had not, after all, gone to the same courses or college; so I wrote them, and went with relative serenity through the following years. No, that's not true, the serenity. But the weather changed for me. And the fact is that, had there been nothing to rewrite, I would have been stranded. I would have become, well, I don't know, someone with whom to avoid eye contact, on the subway or the street.

But here I was, twenty years later, with six papers overdue, and this time there was no way for my brother to write them. So I did the uncharacteristic part. I went to a hypnotist, a Chinese hypnotist. Well, I almost did not go, but when somebody gave me his name and phone number I made an appointment. The voice at the other end of the telephone line was oriental, and the name, as I understood it, was Dr. Hoy Lee. By the time I decided to cancel, I had lost the number, there was no Dr. Hoy Lee in the phone book. I kept the appointment. The doctor was oriental but his name was Hoyle Leigh. What makes you think I can help you? he asked. I said, Well, you can help people to stop smoking, to lower their blood pressure. It is not a reasonable expectation of life to write sonnets, but it is more natural than not to write papers for school.

He said, all right, but no more than one visit, two visits at most. The odd thing was this, it almost worked.

The truth was, there was something in the ice cube. I don't like this mode. Tell about the scandal at the tennis courts, Smiley, the handgun. Helplessness, your professional capacity. I mean, has she no occupation, what does she do for a living? Well, she frets. Fretting is not an occupation. Yes it is; for a spy, a reporter, a scholar, many people. Dayshift. Nightshift. Watchers of soap operas. Can the Rich Write. Tell about lunch with the vedette; and Ben, and the garland, and the swami with the baby in his arms. And, in the matter of the Irish thing. But do you sometimes wish it was me?

The punchline can remain in families when the joke, such as it was, has long eroded. Where is my poison, my father used to say, every single morning, as he took the mild medication that had been prescribed for his arthritis. He believed his tablets to be very strong, however, and took them with considerable ceremony. Where is my poison? he would say, quite loudly, and my mother would hand him the small bottle of pills. One weekend, in my junior year at college, Sally came to visit. At breakfast, we spoke of the dog, Bayard, the Great Dane; never having been much of a watchdog, he had barked a bit the night before. Where is my poison? my father said, and Sally, who was in considerable awe of him already, leaped to her feet and, crying No! upset her cup of coffee.

Long years later, in fact quite recently, I had what may have been a similar misunderstanding, though without, so far as I could tell, any ingredient of horror. I was in an English country house, on a shooting weekend. Everything, the house, the trees, the countryside, the dogs, the river, was beautiful. The retrieving dogs were all enormous Labradors. The hostess's personal pet, however, was a small, golden spaniel, which for the most part trotted by her side. Several times, the lady mentioned that this spaniel's front teeth were missing. I felt some response or comment was expected of me. She had found these teeth embedded in the rear end of a three-legged greyhound, another of her pets. She found it remarkable that so small a spaniel should manage, or even try to bite so much taller a dog as this three-legged greyhound. When she actually bent down to show me the spaniel's jaw, where the teeth were missing, I asked, Did you remove them? Heavens no! she said; it's congenital, a calcium deficiency. And I realized that she thought I had asked whether she had removed the fourth leg of the greyhound. No, No, I meant the teeth, I said; did you remove them? And she said, Why yes, as soon as I found them. But the exchange was relatively calm.

Here's how matters stand at the tennis court. I have played there since I was ten, when there was just one court, outdoors, clay, surrounded on three sides by a wire fence. Now there are five courts, one under a large wooden structure, two under bubble tops, and two outdoors between the old court and the long, sloping meadow, where the backboard used to be. The meadow stretches some distance, right down to the firehouse. All the town's ambulances are still run, not out of the hospital but out of the local firehouses, and manned not by doctors but by firemen. Two years ago, I came into a little house where the court phone and office and showers are, along with the Coke machine, on top of which there is a television set that kids of the players, kids of the pro, kids waiting for lessons watch all day long, I walked in and saw on the couch a man so pale, and obviously ill, and sweating that I asked at once whether I could do something, and only realized seconds later that I knew him, that he was Morty Stone, the young internist who, when he first came to town, brought with him, along with his clear contempt for the local general practitioners, the modern notion of telling people, frankly, whether they wanted to know or not, what the prognosis was, whether they were dying, along with the old commitment to keep them alive, by whatever means, at whatever cost and in whatever pain. There was Morty, then, who had treated my grandmother, in fact, and wanted to tell her the worst and then operate and hold down on the drugs, but who was, quite simply, overriden by Dr. Mills, our family doctor, in actual charge of the case. It was Morty, then, who lay there. What he had done, actually, was just to dislocate his shoulder. The friends, all doctors, with whom he had been playing, were out on the court again, where, with the fifth of their group, they had resumed their Wednesday doubles. I thought this heartless of them, but they had done what they could for him, and I guess they could not bear to watch him now, with that look, the cold, the unmistakable pallor, of a man who, though his injury is minor in every sense but one, is badly hurt. He didn't want company in any case. What he wanted, all he wanted, was morphine. The pro's young son had run to the firehouse, the ambulance was on its way; in due course, Morty was on his way to the hospital and his shot of morphine. I don't know whether or how it affected his dealing with patients, but I suspect Morty had never been in that kind of pain before. In any event, though he dropped in at the court three days later, with his arm in a sling, and though he had played every Tuesday and Thursday for years, and though the injured shoulder healed completely, he never quite brought himself to play tennis again. Never to this day, I mean. Maybe someday he will start again.

But now, here's how matters stand at the tennis court. There is the scandal, in which all of us are, to some degree, taken up. And at the firehouse, there has been a tragedy in the course of which two men, the first in the town's history to be killed in the line of duty, are, as it turns out, with perfect futility and for no reason, dead. The two men, friends since high school, were in their late thirties, legendary. One had been a football hero; the other, the smaller of the two, was famous, miles around, for this: he was able to eat eleven wieners in twenty-two bites. The way the two men died was this. A roof and three floors of a factory fell on them. They had gone in to rescue a man who ought to have been in there but was not. And in the matter of the Irish thing.

I said, But can we live this way.

A moment here. A moment here for a topic. Sentimentality in the work of Gertrude Stein. A real contempt and aversion for sentimentality, too, of course, an attempt to expunge the conventional and easy from her work. But, say what you will, A rose is a rose is a rose is not an unsentimental line. All right, on the other hand, Thomas Wolfe. Obviously, unremittingly, concededly sentimental, *Look Homeward, Angel, You Can't Go Home Again.* But Gertrude Stein, I suspect, rather despised her life, and Thomas Wolfe was rather proud of his. Free of constraints, reserve, hesitations, he was free to go sentimentally on and on. She went on and on, too, of course, but only in a state of tension: drawn to the sentimental rhythm and the sentimental substance, but mocking and concealing it, reining it back. A rose is a rose is a rose is a joke, after all, and a truism, and a pointing out of something. But whatever else it is, it is not in spirit so remote from a stone, a leaf, an unfound door, and all the forgotten faces, which is Thomas Wolfe's. A great hollow wind blows through both of them, and both are on the verge, undeniably, of tears.

All right. I can't read her either.

This is my little disquisition about football: the quarterback, the center, and the towel. On the rare occasions when I went to football games in high school, they were night games. Saturday nights, of course, when it was cold and dark, with a little rain or snow perhaps, while people huddled under their blankets and drank beer. In those days, I wore my glasses only when I had to, and my sight was better than it is now; but even with my glasses on, and no matter where in the stands I sat, I could not see or understand a single play. It seemed to me there were moments when the players stood about, moments when they crouched in opposition, a moment of rising tension, then a thud or scuffle, and they all fell down. After each play, I usually knew what must have happened, either because somebody told me or from the changed position on the field. But that was it. I never saw the ball or knew who had it, even on passes or the longest runs. With television, naturally, I can see and understand the play; and even in the days when I couldn't see it, I had always liked the game. But as often as I've watched football on television, and as much as I've come to appreciate some of the beauty of it, there is always, inevitably, repeatedly, a moment that strikes me as wonderfully bizarre. It is the moment, at the line of scrimmage, when the quarterback wipes his hands on a towel draped over the crouching center's rear. I understand it, obviously; the quarterback, to be sure of getting a firm grip on the football, needs to dry his hands. But, as often as I've asked about it, nobody has gone beyond that explanation, delivered, always, as though nothing could be more ordinary. Whereas what interests me, what I simply cannot imagine, is how the particular custom came into existence, the history of it, the history that is, of the quarterback, the center, and the towel. My brothers admit that they remember no such custom in their day, others have said the same. Was there, then, a moment, on a very wet day, when the first quarterback, muddy and soaked through, saw no further avail in wiping his hands on the back of his own uniform? The ball kept slipping out of his hands, say. Then, the center having perhaps been injured, another center, in a fresh, dry uniform, ran out onto the field, crouched at the line of scrimmage. This happened, perhaps, many times. Many times, on soaking wet days, with second-string centers in fresh, dry uniforms, quarterbacks began, perhaps absently and in desperation, to wipe their hands on the back of the centers' pants instead of their own. And the first center, or perhaps many centers, startled, said, Hey, cut that out; or perhaps, though they were not startled, they were embarrassed; or with the advent of television, somebody, the center, the quarterback, the coach perhaps or the television producer, thought it looked embarrassing, maybe that's what happened, to have one man wiping his hands on the seat of another man's uniform. Or maybe, since the first-string center, presumably as wet as any of his teammates, could not serve in this drying capacity, maybe someone thought long and came up with something dry, a towel. Where to put it? And the answer was what we have. Or maybe the first quarterback said to the first center, when they were both soaked through, Look, Mo, I know this sounds silly, but could you carry some Kleenex or something? And Mo said, Are you out of your mind? The fact is, I just can't imagine it. The conversation that produced the first few instances of what subsequently became that particular custom on the field.

Look here.

This is about the old couple, weaving back and forth across the road, looking for eagles, who told us about the air controllers' strike.

Before I resume my torts songs, I'd like to mention what I did not always know: what an act, what a prolonged state, of bitterness, hatred, stamina, rage, grim aggrieved persistence it requires to sue. More often, people mention money. It is true that, here, lawsuits are expensive. In Germany, a woman leaning over her back fence insults a neighbor with an epithet. The neighbor sues for slander. At issue may be twenty marks. The loser pays the winner's legal costs. The lawyer takes his cut. And that is that. Here, on the other hand, with an ingenuity that should take an entrepreneurial schemer's breath away, there has evolved the following proposition: that a legal job no sooner comes into existence than it generates, immediately and of necessity, a job for a competitor. I can think of no other line of work where this is true. Even in something as apparently two-sided as, say, tennis, where you would think one competitor's initiative inevitably entails work for another, there is not the same degree, or relation, of necessity. It is always possible, that is, that a tennis player will serve a ball and no one will return it, or issue a challenge and no one will respond. But, if a lawyer has been employed to sue, you must employ another to defend, or else you lose. And to have such a profession highly paid, and paid for the most part not on commission but by the *hour*, meaning the longer it takes the more it costs, with no objective measure (as in mining, say, or the construction of a house or of a coronary bypass) of just how much work is done; well, it is a dream.

Freudian analysis had, for a time, its own inspired market thesis: that the cost was part of the treatment; that part of what you were paying for, in other words, was the overprice. And surgeons are thought to be well paid, particularly when the surgery is unsuccessful and the patient dies. But in neither case is what the professional is paid to do the undoing of what is being done, at the same time, in the same forum, by an equally well-paid professional. And even in fields where there exists a symbiosis, or at least an ambivalent dependence, between what are, professionally, antagonists— crooks and detectives, prisoners and prison guards, in one sense social workers and the poor—the dependence is one way. Detectives and prison guards need criminals, social workers require that people should continue to be poor; there are, in short, many workers with a vested interest in the failure of institutions that employ them, and in the insolubility of problems they are paid to solve. The perfect instance occurs in the narcotics laws. A substance, cheap to manufacture, is addictive. It is outlawed. Being outlawed, it becomes rare and expensive. Immediately, and for the first time, it becames profitable for someone, the seller, to make people addicted to it. The law generates a criminal apparatus which in turn generrates a law-enforcement apparatus. With time, their personnel become the same. But the nearest analogue, as a business, to the law lies not in business but in the military, as it prepares for war. If I build a bomb I virtually assure that my adversary must build a bomb; but no one would maintain that anything valuable, conceptual or moral, within our system rests upon this symmetry, as it is said to rest on the adversary system in the law. Last year, the amount spent on lawyers in this country was approximately eighty billion dollars. Much more, of course, was spent upon defense. Whose voice is this? Not mine. Not mine. Not mine.

I said, But can we live this way. He said, I don't know, but it's too bleak. I'm here and you are gone. I just can't let it happen. I said I can't, either. But do you sometimes wish it was me? Always.

Here's how it was: the ice in my drink at the radical lawyer's house was melting. It was night, after my usual bedtime. I was having vodka. He was drinking coffee. His wife and the two others had their herbal teas. And the ice cube in my drink, I could not help noticing, was murky. I mean, apart from a kind of frost around it, there was, unmistakably, a speck of brown. Ice cream, I hoped. A little melted chocolate ice cream, spilled over perhaps from its cardboard container, frozen now into the cube. But as the ice continued melting, and whatever it was come closer to dissolving in my vodka, well, I thought, this is a radical house of late-night coffee and of herbal teas. When I was offered a vodka and accepted, I should have known I took my chance. But then, of course, I thought I'd drink it down before it melted, while the drink was clean and still transparent. But I didn't. What the hell. And somehow, amiable, pleasant, interesting as the conversation was—about terrorism, about the passport cases—I hoped that there was something about which we might genuinely agree, one subject maybe that mattered or did not matter equally to us both, and on which we could be, how else to put it, friends. So I said, about those

witnesses before congressional committees in the fifties, why is it
that every book and article calls them informers? It seems such a
hard word. I mean, regardless of what they said or didn't, they were
witnesses, under subpoena; informers suggests something quite
different, a betrayer for instance in one's midst for pay, as in Ireland
say, in those days. And the lawyer, and more emphatically his wife,
said, But you don't realize how many people's lives were ruined.
And I thought, Still, still, there must be a safe harbor for us in this
conversation. In the end, there was, a safe and uneasy harbor; we
got there the long way round. But in the meantime I had said, I
think truly, I was trying to keep it true, Didn't we, or most of us,
in those days, think of government in another way. I mean, we
assumed it was for us, it was trying to do the right thing. When
the state came and said, for instance, to my parents, you must take
that spillway down and lower the level of what had been a beautiful lake by four feet, you must do it for safety reasons, my parents
would never have questioned it. They were appalled to think it
had been unsafe, that people were imperiled by it. And they took
down the two-hundred-year-old spillway at once and without question. Now, now we know better, that the state was not at all benign
in this and not concerned with safety, and that the Constitution
even foresaw this, foresaw that the state itself is what citizens must
be protected, by law, against; and now we know we should have
resisted by every legal means. Now, we may even be able to restore
the beauty of the lake. But then, in those days, we trusted. That
idea is embodied for me in this, that in those days a lady on the
train said to me that if I got lost in the city (it was my first visit by
myself), I must ask a policeman. Ask a policeman. A policeman.
And of course, in due course, I could never ask a policeman in, say,
Neshoba County. And, in due course, something happened, not
the absolute deterioration, no, but something happened to that idea
of government, and trust.

So we left it. I mean the witness/informer question, as it turned
out, meant so much more to them than to me that I left it, and they
even came a little bit nearer to me on the question, about which
oddly enough I turned out to care more than they, of terrorism; and
we had always agreed on the passport cases. But I went home sad

anyway, and uneasy. I thought I'd get some milk at the all-night Korean grocery, and then, as I passed my car, parked so legally and felicitously at the curb since that afternoon, I remembered there were some letters in it, which the post office had forgotten to forward to my former tenant. I thought, I hope he's forwarding my letters, if there were any; and so I stopped, thinking, It's time I forward his. I had difficulty unlocking my car door, though, so I put the bag of groceries on the sidewalk, and my handbag on the fender, thinking nothing about it. And I opened the door, and leaned into the car to retrieve those letters. With no sense of threat, I felt a presence, two presences looming behind me. I turned, and they ran. To my amazement, I ran after them, shouting, in a voice I didn't know. Absurdly. Please, stop thief. Running. Nobody so much as turned as we ran, they or I, right past them.

Well, there's all that. But when the two policemen later asked me, in my apartment, Why did you have all those things in your handbag, I could not explain. I said, Well, I live in two places. But I had once, in my way, I remembered, thought it through. My house in the country cannot really be locked. I myself have at times pried open and gone through the window. City apartments; well, even our brownstone has had some of the strangest intruders, including one young white man whom the tenants upstairs saw trying to lever my door from its hinge with, of all things, a piece, a tine is it? of the banister. So I carried the objects I most loved and valued. What I must have thought is, essentially, to get these, if fate wants to take these, it will have me, what can I have meant but my physical person? it will have me to reckon with. So I gave up. And while I was simply enumerating objects, the watch, the tie clip, the krugerrand from the fiftieth anniversary, I suddenly said, And wouldn't you know it would happen after an evening with a radical lawyer? The policemen looked up. They had initially thought, before they asked me that is, that I was a teacher. But now we talked for a moment; and there was the obverse, yet the unmistakable counterpart, of the tension I had felt with the radical lawyer himself, and his wife. I wished, as I had wished earlier that evening, that I could unsay something. Then it seemed all right. As they left, though, one of them said, Well, here we go, the Gestapo after those poor boys from the underclass. Quanta. It's better without the scarf.

I think, Frank said, within two years, we are going to have a little nuclear war somewhere.
You mean a little dust-up.
A little dust-up, with a little fallout.

Every few years, since the early sixties, I have received a piece of hate mail, unsigned, postmarked Bridgeport or Hartford, from Rosalie Kamarski. The letters, on unevenly torn and folded pages of lined notebook paper, are forwarded to me from the place where I lived as a child. My parents still live, in summer, at the same address; and though the rural street number has been changed several times over the years, as the township grew, the number on the envelope is always one digit off what the old address used to be. Some years, the handwriting is tidy; other years, it's a meandering scrawl. But wherever I am, and although I hardly knew her, I have always known, when those envelopes arrive, that the message inside is hers, and that for some reason I have heard again from Rosalie Kamarski. In high school, where the few conversations we ever had took place, Rosalie was a small, dark, rather kittenish girl, with even features and an extremely soft, soft voice. The only indications I can think of that there was, even then, something amiss were the softness of the voice; the fact that, when she had once said to me, softly, reverently, "You know, Sy Misler is a genius," and I had said I didn't really think so, Rosalie, in every subsequent conversation would ask, several times, "But really, why don't you think Sy Misler is a genius?"; perhaps also, that she once revealed to me, smiling, in that voice, that she had a terrible fear of butterflies (but one of the kindest, sanest friends of my adult life, it turns out, has the same fear), and of course that, pretty as she was, by the standards of that time and place, Rosalie seemed to have no friends. Every grade, in every school, in every town, of whatever size, in those days, was said to have its genius; and Sy Misler was generally considered to be ours. I don't know why I questioned it, at least aloud. From Rosalie's insistent returning to the subject, I took it that she was in love. The fear of butterflies

surprised me, as did, in Rosalie's case, the lack of friends. But I had
only one friend myself, and he was at another school, the trade
school. I feared, and generally tried to avoid the central high school.
In a pale green Ford, passed on to me by my brothers, I would skip
school as often as I dared to. And I had, in general, such problems
of my own that I hardly thought of Rosalie as troubled, hardly
thought of her at all. Certainly not as holding any grievance that
had to do with me, except perhaps in the matter of Sy Misler; certainly not as in any way deranged. But suddenly they began, these
letters, arriving at intervals of several years: You cheated in Latin;
We all knew you were going out with a poor boy; We knew how
you used to cheat in Latin; You look old and ugly; I hope you die
soon; Everyone knows. In the early years, I used to keep these com-
munications, for some reason, until I lost them. Then, I began to
throw them out, as soon as I noticed, from the opening words and
the lined paper, what they were. In recent years, I sometimes burn
them. But this morning, after I received and burned one, unread,
I thought, this correspondence is real, these letters always seem to
reach me, forwarded inadvertently from my childhood home.
Maybe, in spite of no return address, Rosalie expects an answer,
an acknowledgment of some sort; maybe she wants to appear in
print; maybe she wants none of these things. But here it is, here
she is, Rosalie. I hope she will stop writing to me now. Are we
speaking of the anti-claque? No, not at all, of an actual person.

They were playing That Was the Night When the Lights
Went Out in Georgia. They were playing Bach: Ich Hatte Viel
Bekuemmerniss. In the matter of the Irish thing. Do you some-
times wish it was me. Always. Pause.

So it is to be another Christmas, then, and another New Year's
on my own. Well, it is all right. I have grown used to it, have come
almost to prefer it. Those days for most adults, it is generally ac-
knowledged, and perhaps for all but the fewest children are so
grim. Along with birthdays and of course Thanksgiving, only
worse. Why observe them, then, unless one is for the sake of the
children, or the office, or someone else's sake, obliged to. Well, no
reason. I remember the years when I used to go, on New Year's

Eve, to the gatherings of that dwindling, aging group of German refugee intellectuals. They drank a little wine, and they ate nuts and those little open sandwiches with anchovy paste or radishes, and like everyone else in the Western world they were looking at the clock. Those occasions were entirely in German, and one year, after several years, Professor Hans Ehrlich turned to me and said, Kate, I didn't realize you understood German. He said it in German of course, and since I could not recall having spoken a word of English at New Year's in that room, I was still taking in that word "understood," when Grete said, Yes, and isn't it a shame; she used to speak it. Only then did I realize that they were hardly aware that all their conversation, when they were among themselves, was in their native language; and that my command of the language, though still easy and fluent, was becoming more overgrown with error over the years. Over the years, too, I became more and more confirmed in a sort of superstition: that I needed to be in bed, and sound asleep, before midnight on December thirty-first. So I would look at my watch, and at about ten-thirty I would say, I must go home now; you see, I have this silly superstition. And every time, every single time, whoever I was talking to would become, visibly, distrustful. What kind of fool do you take me for, they (too) were much too polite to say; you are younger than we, you are going to meet somebody else, you have something better to do at midnight. And I, I of course could never say, If I had something better to do, if there were something better, why would I have come? Well, but Christmas. This year, as in the years going back some time now, I guess I'll not join somebody's Christmas, either some other family's or that group of strays, situated rather as I am, who now travel together to spend their time in New Delhi or at Vail. From the fact that I seem to have that choice, it is clear that I am not at all one of the neediest cases—though, for years, long ago, I may have been, in at least the sense that I had no friends. No, here I am, not friendless, and the choice is mine. Why mention it, then, why allude to it at all. Because it would be part of what I know, part of what I have to tell, that I understand something, not everything, but something, of what it is to be alone. In this way. And that there must be others who are and have always been alone. In this way.

Those for whom there was, first dimly, then more bright, then dimly again, a possibility. Which, though dimly, perhaps still exists, but which they know, have somehow always known, would never come to anything. They were never, how can I put this, going to be a part of life. It is as though, going through a landscape, through the seasons, in the same general direction as everybody else, they never quite made it to the road. Through the years, humanity, like a tide of refugees or pilgrims, shoeless and in rags, or in Mercedes, station wagons, running shoes, were traveling on, joined by others, falling by the way. And we, joined though we may be, briefly, by other strays, or by road travelers on their little detours, nonetheless never quite joined the continuing procession, of life and birth, never quite found or made it to the road. Whose voice is this? Not here. Not mine.

But in London, no, what happened first is that we arrived, one night, at Heathrow. It was my third flight, that fall and winter, standby, New York/London. A day flight. And on the plane, I met Anne and Matthew, friends whom I had not seen in years, since the day they married. Anne had just been in the hospital; so had I. They were returning to England, where they live. That night, as Anne and I were waiting for Matthew to bring their car from the parking lot, we saw two military men, Americans, climb into the back of a large black limousine. When Matthew drove up, and had put our suitcases in the trunk, the limousine still stood there, blocking our way. Suddenly, there were popping noises; and, out of both its front and back doors, arms extended, holding out frothing bottles of champagne. The arms withdrew; they were clearly celebrating in that limousine. More popping sounds, and again the military sleeves, the frothing bottles. We thought they must be welcoming some beloved officer. But then, Anne said, You don't suppose they've freed Colonel Dozier? Not a chance, we all thought; we assumed he had been dead for months. But when Matthew turned on the car radio, it turned out to be true: Dozier freed from the Italian Red Guard. Well, who now remembers Colonel Dozier. But it seemed to us then, in the car, an omen, good in every way.

Can it be done on friendship? I don't think so. On intelligence? No. On hope, on love, on fame, on trust, on family, memory, convictions. I don't know. But if, one day, old, and propped against the pillows, or rocking in chairs together, holding hands perhaps, by the fireside; if, looking back on our lives, older now, looking back on our lives we could say, It was all right, looking back, even the things that looked like mistakes, even the apparent misfortunes at the time, they were not mistakes, they were only part of our lives till now. We have been lucky together. We are drinking, by the fireside, and thinking, why did we worry, what was that remorse. We are here still, and what happened, what we did was right. Then we will have done it. Look here. But can we live this way.

In London, on Hays Mews, in fact, the phone rang. The phone calls began. But, no, in London, as well, an elderly priest made a pass at me. I thought, I must be mistaken, I have misunderstood it, he thinks I'm sad; it is his custom to take sad parishioners in his arms, to console them, but no. There was no mistaking it, a strong, self-confident, by no means repellent or ungentle pass. And I burst into tears. When we had settled then, perhaps more improbably still, on the sofa, with drinks, I said, Father, do you think I should seriously consider becoming a Roman Catholic. He said, Heavens no. I thought, It's come to this. And yet. I cannot explain by what series of misunderstandings, or perhaps not misunderstandings, by what sequence of events we had arrived at this moment. He took out his wallet and showed me pictures of the young woman and small children whom he referred to as his Italian family. He phoned. He even sent a telegram, signed love Father Riley. And yet. Well, what did we do instead, I ask you that, what shall we do instead. But I believe, you know, I actually, naturally think, in long, sad, singing lines.

And in London, there was that lunch, in a small restaurant, with Annabel. I asked about her children; and in talking about her younger son, she said, You know, he flew the other day. I said, Flight school? She said, No, in his meditation, actually. I asked how it was. She said, Well, you know, it rather hurt. I mean, he only rose six inches, and he didn't fly for long. But he's lanky, and as he hadn't expected to fly so soon, he said it hurt rather when he came back down. She was smiling as she told this; I was smiling. But we both believed it, and were pleased for him. Moreover, there has already been a practical application: he meditates with his grandmother, from time to time, and it helps with her arthritis; partly the meditation, in and of itself, but also because, perhaps herself on the brink of flying, she becomes so light.

She said, Of course I haven't left. But she really thought, at first, it was too late, she had been too long alone by then. He said, You see, I didn't know. I said, I would never leave.

This is about friendship and my tantrum and how I both was and failed to be a citizen of my time. The conference on refugees was meeting that week, under UN auspices, in Geneva. We were sitting down to lunch, Diana, daughter Sylvia, a few other guests, and I. John was off covering the conference, which had begun, as international conferences routinely began in those years, by voting to exclude Israel. And Diana's daughter said, in that embittered, bored tone children of highly political parents often have: I suppose, all the same, they'll do nothing, as usual, this year, about the Libyan refugees. The what? I said. She said, still somehow cynical, resigned, pained, complacent, the Libyan refugees. I said, But there are no Libyan refugees. Diana explained that the Libyans are rich, that their country is sparsely populated and rich with oil. Well, then, the Palestinians, the daughter said. There was a pause. Then, Diana, perhaps to turn the bitter tone at least to good effect, said, You know, it's very interesting. People used to denounce hijackings. What they do not realize is that this is the means, by the hijackings and then secret blackmailing agreements with the airlines, by this means the Palestinians have been supporting the people in the camps. Because the camps, as you know, are a UN responsibility. But from the UN they were only getting one dollar, per month, per family. I said, rather mildly, Surely not, surely it was more than that. And she said, No, it is true; I know it for a fact. I said, But Diana, when were the first hijackings, the early sixties, and the UN mandate began in 1948; surely, in the years between, the Palestinians were living on something. And she said, Yes, on one dollar, per family, per month. It is simply not generally known. And as she went on, explaining, as she thought, what had happened in the Middle East, I said, with an inner irony but ashamed of myself for lying this low, It is odd that no one has ever written this history. Diana said, Pierre, of course, will write it, in his book about Israel and the Palestinians. Until now, he has not had time. But, when he has time, he will write it. In his research, at Princeton, he has found many documents, previously unknown. And Sylvia muttered something, which I thought included the word collaboration. I said I hadn't understood. There was a pause. Sylvia said, more loudly, About the collaboration. I said, Collaboration between whom? And Diana said, Well, you see, Pierre has discovered in his research these documents, at Princeton, about collaboration between the Nazis and the early Zionists. I said, Surely, Diana, that would be a considerable scoop, and it is odd that Pierre has not gotten around to it. She said, Yes, it would be of enormous value to the Palestinians. Pierre has simply, so far, not had the time. I said, Look, there are not, there do not exist, at Princeton or elsewhere, previously unknown documents about such a collaboration. It is the most exhaustively, publicly, documented period. Ah well, Diana said, certain interests of course would like to suppress them, but Pierre has seen them; the documents exist.

I should perhaps have left the table then, or minutes before, or never been at the table, but I thought, still trying, there must still be some way, some way to repair this. And one of the other guests said, pacifically, Well, you know, they may not have deliberately suppressed them. The documents may just not have been found till now, in all those boxes. And I said, very slowly, This is the nineteen-eighties, here we are at lunch, but if we are talking about any documents at all, the sort of documents you mean are the Protocols of Zion. Well, Sylvia edged a little away, and the other guests became rather intent on their eating. Diana said, I should perhaps have studied the matter more deeply before I speak, because with your background, your heritage, you would be sensitive to all the implications. And we were, how to put this, we were still at this point, friends. I said, Look, it's not a matter of background. I should hope I would know enough, feel obliged to know enough, about this matter in our century, no matter what my background was. And it went on, this edgy, awful conversation, and the point is, I did not leave. I argued, but I did not leave. Later, when Diana walked me to the courtyard, I was still trying. I said, I'm sorry, your poor daughter, she must have been surprised to have set off such a stormy discussion. Diana said, No, it was my fault; I should have studied the matter more deeply, so that I had the documentation when I spoke. I said, Diana, there is no documentation. She said, again, something about my background. I said, It's not a question of my background. There was, after all, the catastrophe of the six million. She said, Even if it was only three million, I should be more careful what I say. The clear implication of her three million was derisive, as though the actual quantity were fewer and she was being generous. I said, Look, I don't want to haggle over millions. Some people have begun to say that there were no millions at all, that the whole story is untrue, a conspiracy of Zionists and bankers. Now she said, Yes, and in a way I am more concerned with the millions of Russians, for instance, who died also; but who received much less publicity.

He said, Kate, give me your flight number. I'll meet you at the airport. We need to spend some time together. He said other things as well.

This is how it began. The turning point at the paper, as it happened, was the introduction of the byline. There had always been bylines, of course, but only on rare stories and those of the highest importance. Sometime in the early sixties, the paper began to put bylines on nearly all stories, by everyone. No one could have predicted where this would take us. It seemed, at first, a step in the direction of truth, of frankness. Part of every story had always been, after all, says who? But the outcome, in retrospect, was this. From anonymous reporters, quoting, as a matter of the highest professionalism and with only the rarest exceptions, from named and specific sources, we moved gradually, then rapidly, to the reverse: named reporters, with famous bylines, quoting persons, sources, who remained anonymous. There were several results. The reporter himself, with his celebrity, his byline, became in many cases the most powerful character, politically and otherwise, in his own story. The "sources" lapsed, became sometimes highly placed officials floating as facts rumors to which, like pollsters, they wanted to test a reaction, sometimes disenchanted employees or rivals, trying to exact a revenge, or undermine a policy, or gain an advantage, sometimes "composites," a euphemism for a more or less fictional character introduced for some specific purpose of the reporter's own; finally, perhaps inevitably, absolute fictions, inventions of the reporter's to enhance his byline, meet completely new journalistic pressures, advance his own career. Within a period of months, three of the most important newspapers in the country printed stories that were absolute fabrications. The first of these, which invented a child and implied that he was typical of a whole, heretofore unrecognized category of children, was the most obviously false. Any editor, any reader whose intelligence, whose common sense, had not been blunted by the new appetite for this sort of investigation, would have recognized at once that the story was not and could not be true. But first, they tried to get it a prize, and got it. Then they called it a hoax (not the mot juste, surely); and went on to say that the story existed, somewhere, just not in this instance, that they were the victims of on the one hand a hoax and on the other a vendetta, and that they would find the true instance of just such a child. Finally, they spoke of the talent for fiction. What an odd notion it was that fiction was just a matter of getting facts completely, implausibly wrong.

And here we come upon the oddest thing. What it was that people were actually caught at. Falsifying laboratory results. Falsifying medical credentials. Falsifying degrees. Falsifying military records, personal histories. And it was not, it was *never*, though this was supposed to be an era of investigative reporting, it was never journalists who caught the falsifiers at all. And, though this was supposed to be as well, the age of information retrieval, when everybody's records were on file in everybody else's computer, everywhere, people risked their falsifications, and were never caught by computers, either. And, of course, in a way, this was not entirely a bad thing. Because, since well before the earliest days of the republic, it had always been a tradition, first a frontier and then an immigrant tradition, that there should be crannies of identity, that a man should be free to make up, in this free country, a new life and a new name.

Well, sometimes it may be just a matter of hanging around until the breaks can find you. The brakes? No.

This is about a murderer with whom I recently had lunch. I had never met him. His trial had been widely covered in the press. He had been convicted, but not yet sentenced. My view, and Jake's, was that he was guilty, but that the evidence against him had been fabricated; that he had done it, in other words, but nonetheless been framed. The host for this lunch was a designer. He asked me, I think, on an impulse. I hesitated. But what kind of journalist, what citizen of my time am I, I thought, if I take it that just because a man has been found guilty of murder he is in fact guilty; and even if he is, what kind of journalist am I not to see such a person, once, at lunch. I had also this relation with the host, Billy Warren. Eight months before, he had invited me to dinner, in honor of old friends—a couple who were in town only briefly, from abroad. That day, that very day, when I came in from my country house, I had found on the door of my apartment a Notice of Eviction, paragraphs of which had been encircled by our landlady, who had perhaps again been drinking, in nail polish of a particularly vivid red. I was going to take the train back to the country that same evening after dinner. Somehow, I arrived at Billy's apartment early. Well, not early, but fifteen minutes after the time I had been asked for, which in that group meant I was by far the earliest guest. The host was still buttoning his cuffs when I arrived at his door, carrying my little suitcase. I've been evicted, I said, a little breathless. Billy blanched, then said chivalrously, and with real kindness, Do you need money? I didn't, but what a kind reaction, especially since he must have thought from the suitcase that I had some thought of moving in.

Anyway, when I went to Billy's lunch, I arrived fifteen minutes late, and again that was too early. This time, not even the host was there. The cook, or in any event an employee who was cooking something in the kitchen, let me in. The sole of my shoe had been loose for days, now it was flapping. As I waited, it occurred to me to ask the man in the kitchen for some glue. He found some Elmer's Glue-All. I carried it to the living room, to a place well away from the carpets, near a window. I took off my shoe, glued the sole, put the shoe back on. And some of the glue dripped from the sides. With a Kleenex from my purse, I wiped the highly polished floor boards. This left the polish dimmed. It seemed clear to me that a wet cloth was required. Carrying my shoe in one hand, Kleenex and Glue-All in the other, I crossed the carpet back toward the kitchen. The doorbell rang, the door opened, and the murderer walked in. We introduced ourselves. I said, I can't shake hands, you see, because I've been, my hands are. I let that sentence lapse. With shoe back on, and a wet rag in my hand, I returned to the dimmed boards near the window, and began to wipe them off. Though the window was closed, there were some leaves scattered on the floor. I had wondered briefly, when I came in, whether they had blown in earlier, or whether they were from a houseplant which had for some reason been removed. I ignored the leaves, and concentrated on the spot, which was in fact dull, or at least less shiny than the highly polished floor around. Then, I turned to the murderer, shook hands, said, How are you? We sat on a sofa. I asked, Where are you staying now? He said, Well, I'm not in the penitentiary yet. I said, No, I meant was he living in Boston, where his house was and his trial had taken place, or in New York. In New York, he said, I've had enough of Boston, thanks very much. A silence. I said, Does nobody talk to you about anything else? He said, Well, they're going to talk about nothing else when I'm not present, so I might as well talk about it when I am. Face it, you see, I'm a vedette.

They were rich, they were publicly generous. In private they were miserly beyond belief. They were slumlords, but they were on the boards of a lot of charities, and therefore oddly placed to do a lot of good. And this they did. So that, on balance, one has to say, I don't know what. There was all the difference in the world between the beneficiaries of what they were on the boards of and anyone who actually depended on them. They had a meddlesome, inconsiderate, pious, bullying rapacity; and yet they wanted, as a last straw, to be thought poetic. So, one by one, he told the wives of his tenants that he was in love with them. He had no ear whatever for language. He liked to say, I'm very sensitive. Meaning quick to anger. He spoke of heighth, of nucular, of walking with he and I. When his best friend was dying, he said, he's being fed intraveniously.

And I, don't you see, and I, and I. Imagine, if you will, being me.

When one of our oldest reporters, a not untalented man, wrote a long piece, in three parts, entitled Can the Rich Write?, I asked one of my favorite editors why on earth we published it. It's satire, he said. Satire? I said. It's the most slavish, interminable, pointless exercise in snobbery I've ever seen in print. Ah, well, he said, you see, it's satire that cuts both ways. I've had twenty years to think about this, and I know that, whatever the editor can have meant— satire of subject and author, satire of subject and reader, satire of author and reader—whatever he can have thought he meant, there is simply no such thing as satire that cuts both ways.

In the matter of problem one, hope is almost at an end. Well, need it be all or nothing, dear. No, but do you call these crumbs and stale rinds half a loaf? Crusts, not rinds. Crusts. You call this having your cake and eating it? You call this emotion recollected in tranquillity? In the matter of problem two, he does not return our calls. Problem three keeps calling; we have him on hold. Problem four, long-term solutions, there are none. Problem five: we have lost the correspondence, though the subpoena lies here on our desk. Problem six, immediate pleasures, has no active file.

But, look here, my typewriter spoke to me. I mean, I had rented what is called a memory typewriter; I liked it so much that I forgot to read its instructions. When I had typed a page, and pressed the Recall button, what it typed was: "Memo, June 23, 1981: Salary Increases." At another page, "Any of the deferred weeks which have accumulated may be taken in any year, in addition to the regular time scheduled for that year. Pay for vacation actually taken, including both regular and the deferred vacation time, is based on the employee's salary." At every page, there was something from a prior user. Three times, it typed exactly this:

> I have scheduled an interview for you on   at
> If this is not convenient, please let me know so we can make other arrangements for the interview.
> Your application is on active file and available for consideration whenever appropriate openings develoo/   Should a suitable opening become available, we will contact you.
> Again, thank you for your interest in our company.
> We appreciate your interest in our company.
> We anticipate a pleasant visit and look forward to hearing from you soon.
> Please contact our personnel department and arrange an appointment to discuss job opportunities.
> Please complete the enclosed application and return it to us in the enclosed envelope.

Well, I particularly liked the "develoo/"; it occurred in the course of what was evidently, as well, a memo of recommendations concerning Swimming Pool Covers. But I thought, then, of privacy, of thrillers, of secrets, personal and corporate; and that I, too, was about to become a prior user. So, without reading any further, I cleared the memory of all its remaining pages. And immediately, I thought of all that may have been there, and I felt a sense of loss. My typewriter, after all, had tried to speak to me; and I erased it.

At dinner, I said, Can we live this way; what do other people do. He said, It doesn't matter what other people do. I said, I know. You said, What matters now is this.

Here's another sort of thing that happens to and around me. There are five wild cats on our road, three black, one white, one orange. They attack Frank and Marilyn's tame cats, one grey, one calico. One night last spring, Marilyn looked out the window. The white cat was prowling on the hillside. Marilyn heard a flat, understated crack, saw the cat rise and then lie down. Frank had used his rifle, through the window of the upstairs bedroom. I have my own rifle; our whole neighborhood is armed. I would never use that rifle though, have in fact no ammunition. There are vandals here, but so far, though they've stolen weathervanes, smashed some headlights on neighbors' cars parked outside at night, and crushed, as delinquents even in my time used to crush, a lot of mailboxes, I have had no contact with them—except for one foil plate, with french fries and a half-eaten hero sandwich on it, which I found, early one morning, wedged between the screen door and the front door of my house. For some time, though, it has been clear to me that I will buy a handgun. I've known it, in a way, since the night Frank shot the cat.

In the same week Frank shot the cat, Marilyn organized a parade of three- and four-year-olds, on tricycles, on Main Street; Frank and Marilyn bought a hotdog stand on wheels, which they brought home attached to the bumper of Frank's car. It may not, to begin with, seem remarkable that the owner of a kindergarten should organize a parade of very small children on Main Street. But the occasion was Labor Day. The group right behind the tricycles was men on horseback; the group right in front was antique cars. Marilyn had arranged to buy helium balloons for the event, and the woman who brought them arrived, like Mary Poppins, holding the strings of fifty helium balloons and nearly airborne. Marilyn and her partner, Jean, the only other teacher in their kindergarten, tied a balloon to the belt loop at the back of the pants of each child, so that the smallest children, too, seemed nearly airborne. Time passed. The parade did not begin. One child said he needed to go to the bathroom. Marilyn said, Forget it. Another asked how much longer they must wait to start. Marilyn said, Never mind. A half hour later, at ten-thirty, the first groups of the long parade set out, with music and spectators along the route. When the crowd saw the tricycles, cheers went up. The children, heartened, speeded up. The drivers of antique cars were extremely worried as they looked back, not for the safety of the children but that the accelerating tricycles would hit and scratch the finish of the cars. Main Street also has a hill, not a steep hill, but the parade route went down it. Jean and Marilyn, who had not thought of the hill, began, for the first time, to worry. Marilyn, walking backward down the hill, faced the children and made braking motions. Her partner paced the roadside, rounding up and slowing strays. All the mothers who had come were marching, some bearing signs that read We Are the Trinity School. Only two fathers had appeared, both airline pilots, both skeptical throughout the parade and therefore keeping their distance from it. An hour later, when the event was safely over, both pilots shook Marilyn's hand, as though she had made a brave and perilous landing. As she had.

Well, here's how it was about the handguns. I went, in my professional capacity I think, to buy one. In the glass case at the gunshop, there they were. To my surprise, there were so many sizes, kinds, and varieties of them, heavy as tennis rackets, most of them, glistening like snakes. So I turned back. And, embarrassed to leave the shop without buying something, I bought a few periodicals for gun buffs. And many of the articles had to do with the sort of gun you would want your wife to have, if she's alone in the house, and, this is what they call him, the Incredible Hulk breaks in. For months, I thought no more about it. Then, there was another wave of assassinations and attempted assassinations, and I thought, They are going to outlaw handguns, and everyone who should not have them already has them, and, when guns are outlawed, only our side, and I knew in a general way what I thought was our side, only our side will not have guns. So I thought it would be foresighted to buy one, against the day, I vaguely, no, rather distinctly, imagined this, against the day when a call should go out from our side that guns are needed, and that anyone who has one should bring it, at some appointed hour, to some place, or meeting at the corner, so that the people who need them will have guns.

Here's what you have to do in our state: show your driver's license; make a choice; leave a deposit; wait two weeks. The two weeks, presumably, are to check, on the basis of your driver's license, that you have not previously been convicted of a felony. And, I imagine, also, to make sure that you won't do anything on an impulse; that if you are, for instance, very angry, you will have time to cool off. Would you like a new or used one, the clerk asked, when I had chosen one of the less heavy revolvers. New, I said. Well, he said, used is cheaper, and the used ones come from police departments, when they change the specifications. All the same, I said, I would rather have one that's never been used. More than two weeks went by, but when I called to inquire whether I might wait a few weeks more, the clerk said no, the permit to buy expires after five weeks, and you have to start the whole process again. I went back to the shop, paid, decided to buy no ammunition. The clerk put the gun, in its box, in a white paper bag, the flat, white paper bag stationery stores use. I have put the white paper bag, with the box and the gun in it, into a closet. And though there is no ammunition, it seems to me to lie there, ticking. I mean, I know I ought to throw it out. Or not worry about it, after all, everybody has them. And cars are dangerous, germs are dangerous, writing is dangerous, and reviewing is dangerous, and editing is dangerous, and some of those doctors were. So I'm not a coward or a hypochondriac so much, with respect anyway to risks of certain orders. I've taken on a bully or two, in my professional capacity, and on occasions of another sort risked my physical self. But this buying of a gun, this simple, in some ways quotidian purchase, is the most extreme, the worst, most extremest, I can't find the word for it, thing I've ever done.

One of the times he was on his island, and before she ever left, she wrote a story. He said, Kate, will I like it. She said, I don't think so. He said, I won't read it then, if you don't want me to, since it is not in your name.

Here's how it is with the old couple. It is his second marriage. He is a doctor. He married her when his first wife failed, as so many of those refugee wives failed, to make the transition with him across the abyss of culture and of war. But now here's how it is with the old couple, in their second marriage, for love. At bedtime, she likes to watch television, programs he especially despises. He cannot sleep with the TV on; but every night, in the course of the program, she goes to sleep. When he gets up, to turn off the set, she is furious. Either she insists that she was not asleep, and that she wants to watch, or she reproaches him for having switched the set off. You woke me up she says, with rage.

As a child, Jon was told by his parents to live by four maxims:

do the best you can; never boast; never complain; and always think of those less well off than you are. Very sound precepts, all, moral. They only seemed designed to cut him off from any happiness whatever. He does the best he can, fair enough, the effort. If it succeeds, he should not make it known. If it fails, and fails by some injustice or in some manner painful to him, he should not complain about it. And lest he enjoy, even in private, his moment of success, or, in the other case, his private failure, he is to think at once of others. And not of fortunate others, but of others less fortunate than he. He is a truly good man, but the cost must have been high.

Is he gentle with the children, does he recognize the family, I asked the deputy sheriff from upstate, who said he worked mainly with German shepherds, on drug cases and bar fights, and that he had one for a pet. Lady, he said, when he gets into the car at night, I tell you, he becomes a different dog.

My world, after all, has been, in a way, the newspaper, and all these people; and home, whatever home is, consists of sheriffs, neighbors, lawyers, doctors, ambassadors, editors, senators. Also, of course, come to think of it, now swamis. Last summer, when I broke my foot, and could not drive, on account of the brake and the clutch, Ben drove me from time to time. And we talked. When my foot was better, he drove me, in his own car, as a kind of present, to his ashram. When we got there, I thought, I cannot really say that I understand this, it does not speak to me really, but Ben does seem to have, look at him, rapt, chanting, though he is trained as an engineer, does seem to have a faculty for this spiritual matter; and these people are not Moonies; there is nothing sinister here; it seems gentle rather. On the drive back, Ben said, Kate you, who are always seeing doctors, I know you are skeptical, I was skeptical too, for years, but you who are always seeing doctors, why don't you take one class, just one at the ashram in New York? He gave me a ticket, which admits the bearer to one hatha yoga class. And one day, when there was, as there now always seems to be, this pending question of the surgery, I thought why not. So I called the ashram, and I reached a voice with so Bronx an intonation that I thought at first I had misdialed. But he gave me the schedule of the classes, and sounded so very kind, that at the end of our conversation I asked his name and whether I would see him there. He replied, Yes you will, and I am Vishnu. But then, but then, I never went.

In the matter of helplessness. "This is a final notice," the blue-and-white slip from the telephone company said. If I did not pay the amount below within five days, they would disconnect my phone. After that, if I paid the amount in full, there would be a service charge, to reconnect. As it happens, for once, I had my bank statements in order, and canceled checks to show that I had paid my phone bills every month. When I had called the business office, and been put, as one always is, several times, for long intervals, on hold, I finally reached someone. Mr. Beaumont was his name. Yes, he said, phone company records indicated that five months ago, the company had erroneously twice credited a single check to my account. I said it seemed rather hard, on their part, to expect me to intuit an error in their bookkeeping system, and harder still to threaten at once to disconnect. Oh, he said, those notices go out automatically. I said that, for my own records, it would help if he sent me a letter, and some sort of document showing they *had* in fact credited me twice in error. He said, No, I'm afraid we don't do that. I said, Look, you know, you really must; otherwise, I'm just paying this arbitrary and rather large amount, on the basis of this conversation, and a slip of paper that threatens, without any explanation whatever, to disconnect. Well, the long and the short of it is: they did disconnect my phone. And I thought, I can't. The rudeness of their voices; this is a whole different department, it's bullying and rudeness. And the time I had spent on it. There ought to be more important things to occupy my mind. But I can't pay it, I'd sooner bomb them, I'd sooner lose contact with the world entirely, I'd sooner die. I thought this is part of what being black used to be like, this is part of what being poor is like, this is what being stateless is like, this is helplessness. Then I thought, It cannot be; surely I am not this helpless. And of course, within days it came to me, I am the press.

Well, I got a B minus, in a summer course in Ovid, when the requirement for the doctorate was at least a B. Wouldn't you say,

Mr. Hughes, the head of the department, said, not at all unkindly, that in view of the requirement, this is not quite enough. I mean, a B minus, surely, means at most, and not at least, a B. But surely, Professor Harris, I said, a B minus is a B of some sort. Well, yes, he said. And anything that is another thing can surely be said to be at least that other thing? So he said all right.

Everything changed. Gradually, almost imperceptibly, things changed. Months and months later, he said, Kate, it's time, I think I'd better read it. By then, we had long been to Orcas Island, New Orleans, God knows where. He took the story with him. Some time later, the phone rang. It wasn't you. It rang again; it was you, saying, I haven't finished, but, Kate, the raccoon.

And in the matter of the Irish thing, I waited. I told no one, and I waited. I wondered when they would find the car, I wondered when they would find me, I wondered what the cost would be, and, most of all, I wondered, why did I constantly have the impression they were all in it, and what could I possibly have thought they were trying to frame me for, in this matter of the car. A matter in which I had, after all, instantly and readily admitted that I was at fault. If you're going to settle out of court, a lawyer had once said to me, about a friend who was getting a divorce, think of the maximum you can yield and still be able to sleep at night; if they want more than that, you litigate. I somehow knew, had known from the first, that they would want more than would ever permit me to sleep again. But now, home again, I wondered how it could take as long as this, to find me, to find the car. I wondered what they would say, and what I would say, and whether the ambassador, for instance, knew. And then, one evening, two years after the events, the crime, if crime it was, I was with Jake. He was driving, had been driving for three hours, we stopped at a diner. I thought, there is nothing, nothing whatever left to say between us. He's so tired, I'm so tired, maybe this is boredom; whatever he thinks, I may as well risk it. So I told Jake about the Irish thing, and that, to this day, I simply did not understand it.

Well, he said, the policeman and the truck driver were cousins. I said, Yes, that's how it felt. If not cousins, he said, anyway quite in it together. They were going to split it. But I offered to pay, I said. He said, no, what they were going to say was that you demolished the entire truck. I said, oh. And then, of course, I saw it. No one had any interest in my car, or my fender, or my license, or my offer, or his bumper. The officer didn't want to see the car, or even the truck, because he had, in fact, already called the agency to say that the truck was entirely demolished. And written, to the same effect, in his report. Even the rental agency had not the slightest interest in the fender of my car; the amount was just too small to bother with. And my offer to pay was, for them, simply an obtuse and even threatening development. We could not possibly go together for an estimate about a slightly tilted bumper. They were going to split, officer, truck driver, car rental agency, the price the insurance company—a remote insurance company, probably in London—would pay for the demolition of an immense truck. If I had hit and run, all the better; but I hadn't. And the You have my word was not meaningless. I had his word that it was not me they were going to cheat at all. Later, the disappearance of the car itself, or its abandonment, must have struck them all as providential. Who could know, in a country of such strange angers and conspiracies, who had last driven and then left that car, and for what reason. To the price of an immense truck, they could now add, in all honesty, the insurance on an entire, vanished rental car.

Strange horses my husband is running with, Lady Bird said, at the convention, when her husband was being offered the nomination for the Vice Presidency. Strange horses my husband is running with.

One weekend, Ben told me he might bring a swami to the country, perhaps for an entire week, as a vacation. I envisioned a monkish Indian in saffron robes. I was away that week, but I later learned that this swami spent his week's vacation in mufti; and that, every morning, after their breakfast and their meditation, Ben drove seven miles to the store to buy that swami his *New York Times*. But I thought no more of this until one evening, when I went to a session at Ben's ashram in New York. Ben's actual guru was not present, except on videotape; we watched his discourse, one of his old discourses, by Betamax. But after the chanting, a young

man in saffron robes introduced himself to me, and said, Thank
you for letting us use your television set. I was puzzled. Ben
turned pale. But the swami continued, Yes, Ben will certainly
have told you; one night, when his television set was out of order
we went to your house to watch the evening news. For a moment,
I was beside myself. The television set is in my bedroom. I could
not recall in what state I had left the house. But, having so long
unlearned the habit of sincerity, I simply said, You're welcome.
Later, Ben walked me to a taxi, and since it was unthinkable that
he would have entered my house, of his own honorable nature,
unless he were under a spell, I said very little. But then he said,
Kate, I would never have done it, except that I knew, I just knew,
you would not mind. And he promised never to do it again. And
then, or rather now, just before Christmas, Ben called, from his
ashram, collect, to say that he had taken, within his faith, a new
name. And I said, I'm so glad, I *thought* you were going to do it
this time. Is it all right to ask what it is? And he said Srinivasan.
And it means illumination or radiance. I thought of his pallor and
his blondness. Two mornings later, having gone to the country by
bus, I received another call, collect, from Srinivasan, calling to say
Merry Christmas. And is this not odd, is this not odd after all, since
it is my world.

On my floor of this Upper East Side townhouse, I could hear
music, disco, even reggae, coming through the wall. When I first
moved to the city, I had one room, on the top floor of a brownstone
in the nineties; all I could hear was a little traffic outside, a few
quarrels between our landlords, who occupied all four floors below
our own floor, and the click of the nails of the Afghan hound in
the one-room apartment which adjoined mine, which the young
designer who lived there had cleared of all rugs and furniture and
painted completely black. When this young designer, whom I liked,
and whom our landlady had fallen a bit in love with, to the extent
at least that for the last two years I stayed there she charged him
no rent, when this young designer came, as he often did, to my
room, to complain usually of how matters stood at the department
store where he worked, the Afghan—tired perhaps of the clicking
of his own nails and longing for something muffled, fabric—would

race to my bed and bury himself beneath the down bolster I had had since home, and school, and college. In summer, when the bolster was put away, the Afghan, disconsolate, would try briefly to root for a place under my bedspread, then lapse with his chin on a stuffed, embroidered wingchair, the rest of him on a rug. Slight traffic through the window, an occasional horn; soft quarrels through the floor, the clicking of nails, the creak of a tiny elevator —later, when the heat from the roof became violent, the hum of a portable air conditioner. A few years later, when I moved from that room to a floor-through in the seventies, I could hear not just music, quartets mostly, at all hours, from the landlord, but also, through the wall on one side, big-band recordings from the townhouse of a lawyer, who had been a Republican Attorney General. Later, through the same wall, unaccountably, rock, and even what appeared to be mantras, all night, at any hour. The former Attorney General, it turned out, had sold his brownstone to a guru. Both my landlord and the guru's disciples kept very late, odd hours. Sometimes, I didn't know in those days whose music it was I heard through the wall of that brownstone, whether it was my landlord's or the guru's disciples. Long after that, I moved to a quieter house. At night, apart from regular traffic, there was only this, the sound of a loose manhole cover. Some cars hit it, in which case it tilted up and thumped shut, like the excessively heavy lid of a soup kettle; other cars missed it. An irregular thump in the street, in other words, every night for years.

Conscious, as the youngest child at table, of needing to justify any claim upon attention by making a point quickly; conscious, in the offices of seriously busy men, great doctors, the highly competent or seriously rich, the powerful, of needing to keep the visit short; aware of the limited patience of his older brothers, reticent himself and quickly bored; he became a stellar lawyer in his later years. In the law, as in everything, excellence is rare and often anonymous. And, in the law, as in almost everything, everything is stories. Under the American Constitution, in fact, everything is required to be, at heart, a story. That is the meaning of the phrase "cases and controversies," which is what, alone, the Constitution empowers the courts to consider. The courts may not, that is, consider abstractions, generalizations, even hypothetical cases; they may not render what are called "advisory opinions" as to the legality of any possible situation or contemplated act. The courts may only consider concrete, instant cases that actually, concretely come before them— and even those cases can be brought only by those who have "standing" to bring them, in other words, by the actual participants, with the most vital and demonstrable interest in the case. I may not bring suit, in short, because I think someone has done some injury to my neighbor. Only my neighbor himself can bring that suit. So what comes before the court is of necessity, and constitutionally obliged to be, a story; and the only ones permitted to bring the story to the courts' attention, the only storytellers, are the ones to whom the story happened, whom the facts befell.

I said, Can we live this way. You said, Is it too hard for you this way. Kate, I'll change things, if that's what you want.

A case nominally begins with an injury, for which there exists in the law a kind of remedy, usually financial, but sometimes having to do, rather more brutally, with divorce, separation, incarceration, custody. At other times, more nobly, with rights, to speak, to learn, not to be stigmatized by race, to have one's privacy left, by the state and neighbors both, alone. But even injuries, stories, of the clearest injury by one soul against another cannot, for the most part, appear before the law. Unkindnesses, betrayals, miseries of every sort fall into what may be, we cannot know, one of the most touching categories in, or rather quite outside, judicial contemplation. Failure to state a claim upon which relief can be granted. But if the claim, or rather the complaint as it then technically becomes, can be stated in such a way that courts are empowered to take it up, why, then, there is, immediately, or as the law would have it, in a reasonable time, the answer. The person, or persons, or entity against whom suit is brought, that is, must make an answer or concede the case, and lose it by default. With that, complaint and answer, the story, in at least two voices, irreversibly begins. Sometimes as in what are called class actions, there are transparently many, many voices—one class of persons suing on its own behalf and on behalf of the larger class, which includes, however anonymously, what are called all other persons similarly situated. Sometimes, more rarely, most of the story of which the case consists is something to be warded off, in that special kind of suit for equitable remedies called injunctions. To enjoin my neighbor, though, from doing something which the law does not explicitly prohibit, and even from doing things which the law firmly does prohibit, I must prove that not so to enjoin him would result in my sustaining what is called immediate and irreparable injury. But though you may do me just such an immediate and irreparable injury, for instance, by leaving me, or do your child just such an injury by turning the lights off when he fears the dark, the courts will not, in fact are not permitted to, take notice of the matter. And even if I know to a virtual certainty that someone is about to commit what is, quite technically and literally, an illegal act, even a crime, I cannot normally persuade the courts to let me argue that he should be enjoined from going through with it. "A man must act somehow," Justice Holmes, quite often though by no means always cruel in his decisions, said; and our system favors leaving people free to act. If they choose to act illegally, they simply face the consequences of having done so. So, in one sense, every law is simply a codified injunction to prevent everyone from doing the illegal thing; while what are called injunctions are more rare, more narrow, more particular: this neighbor shall not build this dam this high lest his neighbor suffer the immediate and irreparable harm of being drowned. And in that same, broader sense every case or controversy, no matter how immediate and personal it may be, is a class action. Because every subsequent case that is in every key respect similar to it must be decided in the same way, and is therefore decided by it.

I said, I thought you wanted me to go. He said, No, you didn't, you couldn't have thought that.

And here, in a most extraordinary way, the stories told by lawyers, in other words before the courts, differ absolutely, almost perfectly, from the stories told by writers. Because in the telling and the resolution of stories in the law, lawyers and courts alike devote the most remarkable effort to saying, in effect, that the story before them is not new. "It is well settled" or "It has long been decided" is the court's way of trying to conceal that what it is about to say is, in fact, entirely new; otherwise there would not be this specific plaintiff, this specific defendant, these specific witnesses, this set of facts before it. "We have always said," the Supreme Court says again and again, introducing the most radical innovation or regression. With precedents. How heavily and necessarily the courts must rely on what can never be quite perfect precedents. It is as though a storyteller were to say, Listen, please, while I tell you just the story I told last night and the night before, and that differs in no way from the one told by others and before my time. Which is a fine and venerable tradition of storytelling. Except that the courts' version of it has the most radical impulse imaginable on people's lives.

About the story, she had said, It's glum. Now he said, It is glum. But he said so many other things. I said, That's a lovable man though, really. He said, No, it isn't. Long ago he said, This is what matters; what you don't realize is that all the rest is only motion. I said, Emotion? He said motion. There we were. Then, you said, in that voice, It's a love letter in a way. I said, What else is it. So here we are.

But the essential storytellers at the drab, frightening, but sometimes heroic, poetic hearth that is the court are, not the lawyers or the judge at all, but the plaintiff, the defendant, and their witnesses. And these, these almost never understand what is being asked of them, what answers are permitted, what is the point of what is being asked. And nobody in this place, least of all that strange audience that is the jury, understands this incomprehension. *Just* when plaintiff, defendant, or witness thinks he or she has the hang of it, begins to reply, sometimes, triumphantly, sarcastically, in what he or she takes to be the lawyers' language, there is objection after objection from interrupting lawyers, reprimands from judges. Why is it, the lady in the divorce proceeding wonders, that her husband's lawyer can ask her, in scathing and insulting tones, And on the morning of July twelfth, did you not buy three shirts at Bloomingdale's? On the same day, did you not also buy sheets at

Bloomingdale's? And is it not true that on that afternoon you also purchased stationery at Bloomingdale's? And he can do this by the hour, and the judge, having said a few times, Counsel, I don't want to tell you how to run your case but I think your point is established, now appears to be asleep. As does the other attorney for her husband, as do her own two attorneys, while this man drones on in this terrible insinuating way, about what she bought and charged and where, endlessly. She is permitted, it seems, to say only Yes or No. After a while, she thinks she has it. She says, Yes, counsel, as I think I have already indicated to you. She looks to the judge for approval. Nothing. It goes on. Suddenly, again, she thinks she has it. But these don't show, she says, flushing, these lists of my charges don't show the items I returned. But she really does think she's got it, the point, the language, they are trying to put something over on her and she will not have it. But, your honor, I object! she says. These do not show which, if any, of these items I returned! Nothing. She doesn't understand it, doesn't understand that she doesn't understand it. After a while, the judge stops reprimanding her, she thinks the story is now going her way, keeps saying her charge account bills don't show what she returned.

You said, We can live this way. You said all those other things. We do live this way. We just need something to tide us over the pitch, the daily pitch of not knowing whether one or the other is going to go. But now you said, again, Kate, I'll change things, if that's what you want. And, in that voice, It's a love letter in a way. And I said, What else is it. So here we are.

The education and the language of judge and lawyer alike are so remote from the language of the story's own characters that they have forgotten what it's like not to know what is asked, what is permitted. And the jury, if there is a jury, doesn't know either. And yet, the great doctrines of finality and *Stare Decisis,* that somewhere a story must end and may not be reopened, and that this story is dispositive for all stories that cannot be proven to be unlike it, mean that no stories, no stories at all, can be of more immediate, and sometimes eternal, interest than these. But stories they are. And their own eloquence grows up around them. The outcomes, surprisingly often, are wrong. You can see it. A hundred years later, the court sees it and reverses, not reverses, overturns, but comes about like a great ship. Never apologizes. Simply brings in another "It is well settled," along with "What we decide today is nothing more than." Everyone once intimately concerned is long dead. In the process, in the repetitions and formulas, the courts sometimes rise from their droning with a phrase so pure, deep, and mighty that it stays. It remains forever just the way to say that thing. More probably than not. Utterly without fault. Not my act. Beyond a reasonable doubt. Last intervening wrongdoer. Cloud on title. An ordinary man. A prudent man. A reasonable man. A man of ordinary intelligence and understanding. Wait, wait. Whose voice is this? Not mine. Not mine. Not mine. Res ipsa loquitur. A man must act somehow.

Jon's run: The forward-directed attitudes, I think, are these: curiosity, ambition, love, courage, hunger, duty, rage. They may be backward-formed, but they are forward directed, moving toward the future. Fear, too, of course, is forward. No one is afraid of yesterday. Backward-directed are all the loss reactions. Grief, of course, and regret. Boredom is backward and forward, both. Hope. Wait, wait. Not here. Just stay.

But you won't go? No. Never? No.

Do you sometimes wish it was me?
Always.
Pause.
It is you.

A NOTE ON THE TYPE

The text of this book was set on the Linotype in
Fairfield, the first type face from the hand of
the distinguished American artist and engraver
Rudolph Ruzicka. In its structure Fairfield dis-
plays the sober and sane qualities of a master
craftsman whose talent was long dedicated to
clarity. It is this trait that accounts for the trim
grace and virility, the spirited design and sensitive
balance of this original type face.
Rudolph Ruzicka was born in Bohemia in 1883
and came to America in 1894. He designed and
illustrated many books and created a considerable list of individual prints—wood engravings,
line engravings on copper, and aquatints.

This book was composed by The Maryland Linotype Composition Company, Baltimore, Maryland. It was printed and bound by The Haddon
Craftsmen, Inc., Scranton, Pennsylvania.

Typography and binding design by
Dorothy Schmiderer